The *Splendor* of
Antiquity

The best scientist is open to experience and begins with Romance: The idea that anything is possible.
Ray Bradbury

As time passes, we put to memory the history of our souls. Therein lies the splendor of who we are.

To Everyone I have known and loved…
You are forever etched into my soul and will never be forgotten.

Cheryl Anne Gardner

The Splendor of Antiquity

A
Twisted Knickers Publication

1

To Dance with the Dead *in the Fell Moonlight*

My beloved Joliette had long ago stopped living. Yes, death had us both, but even in death, passion knows no bounds. She would love me in the end. For it was just in her nature, I suppose. To love the dead.

Everything dies. The birds, the bees, the trees, and the seas, the earth, the moon, the stars, and the sun — all their times shall duly come. It is ironic, is it not, how everything seems so poetic in death, yet we rarely see the poetry in life?

Death: The moment when pride and vanity abandon us. The moment where humility is our only saving grace. The moment where begging doesn't seem so beneath us. Unpleasant, yes. A grim and unavoidable fact, inarguably, and yet, there are those who would argue, those who would spend long grey days in torment, uselessly obsessing over the thought of their own mortality as they try in vain to knit their will back together with filaments of labored breath. For that lot, death is a terrifying certainty. Condemned not to the material world, it is a certainty that spans the depth and breadth of all life as we know it. The tangible and the intangible alike stumble haplessly into its needful grasp at some point or another. Even the strongest most deliberate of minds will never be able to fully comprehend its reach. Hopes, dreams, aspirations, love, relationships. The very distasteful idea of civilization as a whole, its dogma and its ideals have perished an infinite number of times over the course of history. As the passing of the world slips down through fractures in the muck-covered gravel of time, everything is absorbed into everything else. Every bit of matter, whether it be rock, stone, or bone becomes a part of antiquity. Mist, magic, or trembling lips, everything transcends in an elemental eclipse.

Everything.

Every atom, every slight or obtuse particle of dust, and every swirling cloud of detritus will eventually possess the memory of everything else, etched into its core.

My Joliette understood all of this. Understood it well enough not to realize that its truth had been gnawing away at her for a lifetime.

Her childhood, such as it was, was not so different from any other, she would say. Carefree days of laughing and frolicking, sun-drenched meadows, and the stagnant mire of childhood dilemmas had passed mutely into the history of her life. A history all too brief and burdened with the overwhelming eventualities of death.

Over the course of a lifetime, one might never be able to calculate how many tears could be shed on account of death before one becomes accustomed to it. How many would it take before the pain ceases, before your heart grows cold with acceptance, and how many would it take before you are no longer able to feel anything at all?

For Joliette, it didn't take many.

Mercy's gift, a flood of tears, or so Joliette had always wanted to believe, abacus in hand, as she knelt down and looked out over the edge of the fortress she had built to protect her from the sadness that is death. A jagged edge — steep. An edge where chill winds scour the soul, its lamentation quick and deep. The edge of infinity, some might say, one devoid of idolatry, whereupon reaching dizzying heights, she could stand perched precariously upon a life full of truisms and negate her own desire. Anger, pride, sorrow. Infinite were the blocks of stone surrounding the heart of my beloved Joliette, infinite the rhyme and reason. Joliette's stone blocks were infinitely stronger, as well, stronger than were those surrounding my own decayed body, and so they should have been enough to protect her. But most days, for Joliette, they were not.

I met my beloved during an archaeological excavation high atop the ragged mountains off the coast of the Black Sea. For two long years, she had suffered the encampment, suffered and struggled against forces, which had without abate, endeavored to damn her soul. The elements, the vicious clamor of the naysayers, and the treachery of her own deteriorating self-confidence ravaged her by night and by day.

"The search is not futile," she would say through clenched teeth to anyone within earshot. "I know he is here. I can feel him ... just behind my eyes."

My Joliette could feel me. An ache in her heart. A crimson heat in her stomach. Despite the well-rehearsed cold candor, the impudence, and the rather antiseptic approach to her own emotions, she boasted an uncanny ability for unearthing burial places. It mattered not how old, decrepit, or deeply hidden they were, she always knew. It was as if she could sense them through the shadows of obscurity just beyond some invisible plane of existence, beyond the very corporeal restraint of logic.

For an archaeologist to possess such a talent was quite a boon, and such an extraordinary boon could not have been bestowed upon a scholar of greater merit. Early in her career, her insights and findings had caused a great deal of disturbance in the scientific community, and the moniker rewarded her for her diligence was gravedigger. Although in backroom conversations, the term was used to describe her talents a bit more callously. Joliette wasn't blind to the insults, but she took an unaffected approach to her work, at least to all appearances. She practiced detachment with the discipline of an executioner. Always the socially accepted smile upon her face, the required acquiescent gleam in her eye, and the resolve of cold steel edging against her spine. Their mockery mattered little. She knew the Black Sea would prove them wrong, would prove them all wrong.

And so through the twilight, through history's history, its rubble and its tattered pages, she had come to this place. This hostile, wild, and isolated place. Very much determined she had come, and very much alone. Her colleagues would mock her. Their sharp words set about to cripple her in heart and in spirit, and the mountain would seduce her and break her for it. But Joliette could bear the pain. Tempered by sorrow, she could all but refuse it.

Broken, shamed, and ridiculed, she fought without

relent against all the invalidated assumptions and the apparent pointlessness of her desire. Of singular purpose, she had no choice in the matter. The labor was backbreaking. The terrain, treacherous. But for her, it was a labor of pure love. Worth the sweat, worth the blood, and worth the pain, the persistence of the rock grinding the flesh of her fingers down to the very bone.

As I begin this story — the story of a memory — there were but two months remaining for the excavation. The funding had run out, the patience of the benefactors had been depleted, and so had Joliette's resolve, but on this one night, well into the twilight, with only the onyx ebb and flow of the silent sea in the distance to comfort her, she continued to dig.

Against a blackened sky, the leaden mist had thinned to a dread whisper, drifted away, allowing the sharp bitter light of the moon to obliterate all the stars and penetrate even the deepest recesses of the twilight.

It wasn't the faint embrace of the moon that had awakened me as it bore down upon my grave. No. It wasn't that at all. It was something much softer than that. Much, much softer, and so I turned my ear towards it, towards the dulcet melody of an angel in a dream, and in the darkness my heart was lost.

Yes, it was a desperate breath, mingled gently with the sea air, sweet and poetic. It was the voice of love and longing, and it rang out through the cavernous depths, penetrating the rubble, rousing my spirit from its rocky, black tomb.

I loved her instantly, loved her beauty, her grace, and her strength, and I hoped that she would love me. Love me more in death than anyone ever had in life, but alas, I was a fool.

Hope is the domain of the living.

No one would love me.

A monstrous apparition, how could anyone love me? Formless, timeless, nothing but decay and conjecture. It was impossible, and at the thought of my unworthiness, a long isolated rage coursed through my tattered flesh and broken bones.

It was then that she touched me.

A touch so invigorating that I discovered to my heart's eternal delight that I had been wrong. A criminal err it was to judge and condemn my own soul. She could love me.

Yes, my Joliette most certainly would love me.

2

Returning to France *and other Academic Pursuits*

W
e survived our return to France without incident, but that really depends on how one defines the word incident. Having my skull separated from my body was an eerie and unpleasant condition to endure for certain, and for equally certain, it was a breach of protocol. However, in spite of all the unpleasantness, the suspect methodology, and the separation anxiety, Joliette's engaging company managed to alleviate any distress I might have been feeling over the displacement of my physical body, so once I had settled in, I enjoyed the journey.

We were en route to the Université de Toulouse-le-Mirail in the south of France, or *le Midi* as the locals would call it. Joliette had completed her doctoral studies there and had subsequently taken a position with the University's esteemed archaeology department, but the city meant much more to her than the title inscribed in fancy calligraphy on her degree. The effortless and swooning way the name rolled from her tongue made the place sound luxurious, academically decadent even. *Le Midi* was her true birthplace, the *terminus a quo* for a life that she could, without argument or sentiment, forever claim as her own, but even without sentiment, I got the impression that Joliette was a bit homesick for something more than the city's eternal opulence. The reminiscences flooding her mind opened up a chasm wide and deep, evoking images so egregiously picturesque and romantic that it was difficult, even for me, to distinguish reality from a fairytale. Delusion was one of her more endearing charms, I might add, and not altogether unexpected.

A willing captive to her own intellect, Joliette had difficulty reflecting the nuances of the world she actually lived in however much she inwardly delighted in all its subtleties. Nevertheless, when we disembarked in her beloved city, all pretense was abandoned, and I saw what she saw. Enveloped in the soft pale of dusk, I saw the sweetly scented blush of a rose fall over the city, and the moment Joliette smiled, I knew the tender nature of her heart.

Host to a lush and diverse culture, Joliette's Ville Rose is a city vibrant and alive with color and texture. Whether your heart belongs to art and architecture, academia, or friends, conversation, and good food, there is enough to sate the intellect, the senses, and the soul. The evocative arches of the Pont de Pierre could deliver a weary traveler to the glory of Rome in an instant, but if it's enchanting scenic splendor you seek, fresh air and the irresistible temptation of warm pastries and *café au lai*, then a leisurely stroll through Wilson Square is sure to charm the pensive poet in anyone.

There, the great lyricist Pierre Goudouli sits. Yearning tempered in stone, thoughts lost to the distance, he sits in silence, pondering the pages of his book with scrupulous care. His muse lies by his side in provocative repose, arm thrown over her head as if wounded by the word. Settled snugly amidst a profusion of delights, this garden is an oasis, a brief respite from the humanness of humanity, where miracles come easy, and wonder is but a spire of lavender away. The warm breeze. The hint of citrus hanging in the air as the verdant throws off its dew to the encroaching shadows. Yes, its imagery calls to mind the aesthetic values of the classical romantics, and its poetry exists for no other purpose than to stir the heart and mind to otherworldly pleasures. It was there that we took pause from our journey. It was there, and only there, that Joliette could forget and reconnect her wandering spirit to the present.

"Two years I've been gone," said Joliette distinctly to the statue as she gave herself over to the fountain's refreshing mist. "Two years, Pierre, two years and your words cast crystalline teardrops over her body still. Who says a heart of stone cannot feel desire, even love? Should someone be that ignorant, a moment with you would surely cure them of their ills."

This city was Joliette's Eden, evermore. Once at the center of a vast and expanding Roman Empire, Toulouse had been a key metropolis. Ancient, its imperfections have an almost willful charm. Its magic, its perfume, and its poetry — its whispered kisses, if you will — linger seductively against the flesh, much like Joliette's clumsy words.

"The Université de Toulouse?" she declared later to a curious tourist while he fumbled on the curb for a taxi. "I am heading to *le Mirail* myself. *L'Arsenal?* Yes, that is a lovely campus, too. Humbling even still. So old. So old and so full of history." Without a moment's loss of decorum, she stooped to the pavement in order to snatch up a few notebooks she had dropped, smiling all the while as she blew the hair from her eyes. "The old stone is merely an echo of a time forgotten," she continued with exuberance. "Forgotten but not lost. Yes, that's my pen, thank you. Things just get away from me. Now, where was I? Oh yes, the Université! I am a researcher at *le Mirail*. Archaeology. Anthropology, specifically. We try not to be so clumsy. You must check it off on your map. You won't regret it. The *le Mirail* district is an architectural wonder in itself. I could give a tour. I've been away too long, much too long. It's so nice to reminisce…

"The Université, you see, was established in 1230 and is actually split into separate campuses, not unlike the medieval universities of Oxford and Paris. Have you been? No. Well, never you mind. Some day you might. Anyway, dire times then. The crusades would continue unabated for many more years, and the dark was approaching: The Black Death. An Italian chronicle said, 'They died by the hundreds, both day and night, and all were thrown in ditches and covered with earth. And as soon as those ditches were filled, more were dug.' Digging. Humans are always digging, burying that which we have cast away, and desperately seeking that which we have lost. Yes, the Church, what was their part in it, you ask? Good question. The church was digging, as well. Determined to reconcile Greek Philosophical thought with Christian Theology, they asserted academic control by providing much of the financial support to the institution. This was to further their own agenda, of course. Turbulent times, *oui, oui,* they were. Intellectual revitalization it was called. Europeans were just beginning to translate those ancient Greek texts. Revelations comes to mind. Shock, awe, and secrets, you see. Just words, but words that challenged a region's delusional perception of itself and its stale ideologies. Yes, it is ironic in a way. Ideology staler even by measure than todays. Even so, many rose up to accept the challenge, regardless of outworn opinion, and philosophical testimony the likes of Aristotle's would be a clamor heard far and wide. Their words would inspire a new world view, which in turn, led to a new world order, and this, this allowed for all manner of scientific discoveries and advancements in the arts.

"Today, Toulouse is the second largest university city in France. There is much to see, much to do, much I fear might be overlooked. Would you like to share this taxi?" she asked, and the tourist, either rapt by her voice or anaesthetized by the lecture, nodded his head in bashful compliance.

It was her voice, of course. Few of her words had actually reached him, but the words weren't really important. The words, audaciously intellectual and enlightening, made it all the more obvious that this city was pure academic heaven for her, and yet, the effortless and didactic tenor of her voice betrayed a fragile yet enduring passion. It was more than respect she felt for this place. It was love. Love for every eroded cobblestone, every pitted statue, and every crumbling brick wall. An old love, one I could understand. There had been much overlooked of her heart.

In every willful palpitation, her heart hungered for knowledge and secrets as much as mine own had. I knew what that hunger felt like, the pain of it, the futility of it, and Joliette felt it deeply, more deeply than most. When she wasn't immersed in a book, she was busy throwing herself into fits of desperation while pondering the intricacies of household dust. Yes, I understood the ache she felt. In the reign of my youth, which was thousands of years of tears ago, I had been a passionate advocate for art, literature, and academia, and my heart had been equally sentimental. When I wept, my people felt the promise of my tears.

I wept often.

One among many cultural undertakings, I created the first systematically collected library of a sort, where all cuneiform text and artifacts available were gathered, studied, and stored for later research. Sculpture reached its apogee under my rule. Culture and intellect reigned supreme. Yes, there were libraries before mine. Philistine piles of paper they were. Archives. A truly vulgar practice it was. There, potency had been reduced to little more than tattered ideology. There, history had been accumulated without real interest, and in so doing, its poetry had been allowed to languish in the dank, depthless distance. I have always been of the opinion that inspiration collects itself, not out of administrative necessity but out of higher need. A need to connect with the past, a need to seek order in the minutia.

Holding similar beliefs, my Joliette was the angelic embodiment of Toulouse. As she rambled on and on, really to no one, a torrent of warm air from the open taxi window fluttered without shame through the unruly tangles of her hair. Exhausted from her journey, and her own rhetoric, she became quiet. Sun-forged twists of gold taunting the calm of her face, she lost herself in her thoughts as the University came into view. At that moment, I realized that this city was more than a muse. Joliette was no accidental tourist or academic savant. A Toulousiane ingénue, perhaps, her hand gripping the handle of the door with white-knuckle abandon. Embracement absolute. That is what I felt in her every trembling breath, in the subtle flush of her cheeks. I felt the self-sustaining philosophy behind an expertly constructed deception. The only philosophy an orphan would be willing to press that close to her heart.

Ingénue, indeed.

Once upon a dream, the London borough she had for a time called home was a "leafy area," she often said. Invariably though, suburban sprawl had swiftly crept out and away from London's borders, spreading ill will and desiccation. For all intents and purposes, the relative affluence and pretentious charm of Harrow-on-the-Hill had been obliterated as far as she was concerned. Leaf and laughter had faded into the concrete, and the romance and the poetry had faded to memory, which is how Joliette preferred her memory of home to be. Faded.

In her youth, Joliette had been a scrappy, brazen child with exceeding academic promise and an ego to match it. Her primary and secondary school transcripts were impeccable and her test scores — intimidating. In the top five of her graduating class, science was the true love of her life. Somehow, the innermost workings of the universe never failed to fascinate and reassure her restless mind and spirit. Although, however intimidating her intelligence might have been, her childhood had been plagued with a great many people who simply misunderstood her. The misunderstanding may have been jealousy, but in truth, persons having leanings towards all things dead, decaying, and mysterious do not generally have the benefit of an overabundance of like-minded companions. She had a macabre countenance to her nature, which I found to be splendid and endearing. Apparently, I was not the only one who felt this way.

"Exactly when were you going to tell me that you were back?" declared a deep, slightly brusque voice from the corridor.

Joliette looked up from her soaring stack of papers to confront a young looking and remarkably striking Frenchman. A towering sentinel of chivalrous manhood, he stood before us, arms crossed tight over his chest as he leaned in cavalier repose against the doorframe. He smiled to some extent as her eyes met with his. To what extent I could not determine at first glance. Flattered by ebony curls of hair falling soft over his forehead, his face, even with the inconspicuous smile, conveyed a quiet intensity and strength, and his exquisite eyes, hewn from the deepest mahogany, reflected a vast intelligence — piercing and engaging. The sharpness of his jaw, complete with its impeccably manicured moustache and goatee, finished him off to brutal perfection.

As Joliette had explained to me over the course of our journey back to France, Olivier Botton was the French gigolo of the Archaeological world. Gauche, maybe, but judging by his confident posture and his calculated demeanor, I would say the title was justly deserved if not flagrantly self-appointed.

Botton, having also fulfilled his doctoral work at Toulouse-le-Mirail, had stayed on to become one of the principal archaeologists at the University. His specialty, metallurgy, which, as Joliette had so thoroughly explained to me, is defined as the study of the microscopic and macroscopic mechanisms that cause a metal to behave in the way that it does, the cause and effect which occur on the atomic level that affect the metal's macroscopic properties. Simply put, he studied how something as sharp and tempered as steel could be so affected by external forces. Yes, I could see that that sort of knowledge might be beneficial in certain other undertakings, yet Joliette seemed oblivious to the parallel. She confided to me that this particular field of study was his true calling but that his passion lay with the study of weapons. Ancient weapons. One look into those eyes and I could see the parallel in that, as well.

With unfettered ease, Joliette often proclaimed that Botton was "beyond brilliant." I never understood what that meant exactly, but with Joliette, words were a social triviality. The noticeable lilt in her voice made it impossible for her to conceal the great admiration that she felt for this Botton. Her face shone with a humble iridescence whenever she spoke of him, her smile wide and approving, her eyes wet with a hint of melancholy.

I could well understand the reasons behind the reflexive emotional tremor. Botton exuded a heady air of confidence and command. One could not help but admire his audacity. Notwithstanding the dramatic good looks, his self-confidence, underscored further by the severity of the lines on his face and the raging virility of his libido, was unrivalled in its ferocity. It was evident to me that when he set his sights on a particular woman it would be more of a professional assassination than a proper courting. No mortal woman stood a chance, not even one as tenacious as Joliette.

Taken aback by his presence, she wavered slightly and then scowled at him. She was not so much startled by the sight of him as she was annoyed by the distraction. "Damn it, Olie. You scared the shit out of me. Fucking hell. I just got back."

"Oh, come on, Jol. It's been four days already."

I supposed his retort was justly provoked by her tone. She had been back in the city for several days without giving word to anyone, least of all him. Yet, as irritated as he was by her evasiveness, he never for a moment faltered in his purpose. Deftly dealing with any and every obstacle, he took great strides across the room. When he reached Joliette, he wrestled the papers away from her, grasped her head with bold timeworn hands, and kissed her firm on the lips in rebuttal to her protests. She did, however, manage to squirm free of his embrace.

Manic to create a diversion, she began fussing with the reports on the lab table in an awkward effort to avoid his gaze — put some carbon-based distance between them, if you will — and even though she knew success was at hand, she still felt a guilty urge to explain herself. "Don't start, Olie. The freight will be here tomorrow, and, I have stacks of paperwork to finish. The testing and assessments can't begin unless I get all this paper off my desk. I just needed a few days to get things sorted."

Botton decided to press her further. His mettle had been piqued by her indifference, and he knew he just needed to keep her talking. He chose his words with care, "Rumor has it that the find is beyond belief."

"Rumor?" she replied. "Don't you scientists have anything better to do with your idle time? Yes, it is. The gravedigger would like to think that her time hadn't been wasted as idly as yours apparently has." Contemplating her next witticism, she parried by fumbling her way to the other end of the lab table, consequently shoving him aside with her body as he sought to block her path. "Olie, you know … I am so into this right now. I am not intentionally trying to be dismissive. I just can't think straight. I've not slept in days, and I really do have to get started. You know — a million things and there is never enough time."

Once Joliette made use of a cliché, Botton knew the skirmish was over, and so he relented, raising his arms in a feeble indication of concession, which was no more than a farce. He had no intention of conceding. "Ok, Jol, I'll let you get back to it, respectfully, but answer me this first, am I going to be happy?"

Joliette said nothing, and Botton sidestepped the silence with a kitschy grin.

If I had had a physical form with which to express my exasperation, I would have done so right then. *Bête noire.* The Black Beast. That was my immediate thought, and hers, but Joliette had warned me of his egocentricity and his presumptuousness, and she was far too polite to ignore his puerile and selfish question beyond the acknowledged pause.

"Most definitely," she replied after the pause, "just look at the photos." She slid a stack of photographs across the table towards Botton. "We got full armor, Olie, and weapons. His sword is just spectacular. Everything is just…" As the weighty implications of the photographs overcame her, she cast her stoic demeanor aside and smiled.

A smile that struck Botton's ego senseless.

"We should celebrate, Jol. Meet me for a drink tonight? Just one. Early if you want."

Joliette paused before responding. A pause colored with so much cruelty and pain that it made Botton wince. "I can't…," she finally said once the heat had left her lips.

"Look — maybe another time. I have way too much to get started on, and my mind is racing. You go. I will try to meet up with you later. I have to get these reports in. I'm sorry."

Avoiding direct eye contact, Joliette quickly and haphazardly gathered up her papers and hurried from the lab, leaving Botton flabbergasted and stewing in self-doubt, a calamity he felt certain that he did not deserve.

Even so, he held back the urge to give chase. He just stood there, rolling his eyes and running his hands hastily through his hair, which did nothing to temper all the frustrated sighing. I hadn't anticipated Botton's flair for the melodramatic, and even though the spastic mime routine was amusing, it grew wearisome by the minute. Mercifully, Botton also had a sense of timing. Feeling satisfied — his exasperation duly noted, even if it was only to himself — he eventually gave up playing the victim, plunked down onto a nearby stool, looked straight at my skull and said, "Women! I am fairly certain that you, my rotted friend, are quite happy not having to deal with them anymore."

Rotted friend?

I didn't appreciate Botton's tone, and I didn't like him much either. Of that, I was certain. Exaggerated to epic proportions, his insolence was beyond even my comprehension, and his cowardice was embarrassing. Temper tantrums are for willful children and should rightfully be ignored, but for some reason, his mere presence caused Joliette immeasurable discomfort. That, more so than anything else, filled me with a blackness that cored my soul.

3

A Discussion *on Love and Vanity*

———————————————————————

I f there is one thing that all women love to do, it is talk — incessantly — and it is not simply an issue of clarity. Apparently, women resolve their emotions through the act of talking. The act itself pushes those emotions from the intangible depths of the mind into the tangible world, allowing, in a sense, their fundamental aspects to materialize. Logic suggests that if the emotion in question can be heard via the power of scientifically proven sound waves, thusly, it can then be felt via those very same wavelengths, even if no other were present to hear or feel them.

I was present, and since — being a mere shell of my former self — I had naught to do with my time, and that, coupled with the fact that I was enamored with her, made the simple act of listening to her an enjoyable test of my patience.

In general, Joliette was rather abrupt if others were

present, downright belligerent if she were annoyed, especially when it came to her colleagues whom she disdained without measure, but when she was alone with her work, her defenses fell away and her passion lay tenderly revealed. Her very breath was affected by sentiment. Even though she had devoted her life to science, a part of her remained covered in shadow, the part of her that longed for divinity. Joliette had never taken issue with this. She had long since reconciled her beliefs — her faith in logic and fate — but fate had not been kind to her heart, and her faith had suffered as a result of the treachery.

Even the hour betrayed her.

It was late, as usual. Joliette had learned to do without a lot in her life, but she couldn't do without answers, and so her labyrinthine research style often kept her working until all hours. Long after staff and students had retired for the day and long after the plodding echoes of the cleaning crew had ceased their torments, Joliette would sit silent amidst a cryptic patchwork of annotations with only her meandering thoughts and my skull for company.

I don't know what it was about that desiccated hunk of useless bone that could captivate someone with such totality. It seemed absurd, and yet, here was this precocious creature sitting before me, so intent that I could smell the sweat lying against her perfumed skin, dusty and sweet, like dried flowers.

To permit better scrutiny of me, she had lifted my skull into the air for a long lingering moment as if waiting for the almighty cosmos to pass judgment upon it, and when that didn't happen as she had expected, she withdrew her testimony and placed me under a much brighter light.

Through the large magnifying lens, her eyes became huge marvelous spheres of wonder. Those eyes fixed upon me had an intensity I had never before witnessed in a woman. It wasn't idle fancy. There was nothing idle about the way she stared at me. It felt obsessive, as if she were trying to recreate me from some loosely defined notion, and the construct had stretched her mind beyond its limits. She could know me, and she knew it instinctively, so after a while of twisting, turning, and brow furrowing frustration, her face, weary from the hours and the relentless scrutiny, softened somewhat. She removed her glasses, set them on the table, and then she snapped off the high intensity light, sending everything into shadow. Casting a low frequency gloom about the room, the computer screen flickered eerily in the background, and as the darkness pooled around her, she took a defeated breath and then whispered to me an appeal of nothing less than silken words draped over sorrow.

"I have been searching for you forever," she said. "Please forgive me that we have not been properly introduced. I am usually more mindful, but admittedly, I have been a bit off of late. My name is Dr. Joliette Deneauve. It is nice to meet you? Well, how silly of me, we shall have to discover your name, now won't we, and I do apologize for the rude interruption earlier, Olivier can be … let's just say … a bit full of himself."

As her fingertips moved over the ridges of my fleshless face, static sparks of memory passed through her and into me. How could a woman so lovely be burdened with such heartbreak? The pain was significant, the violation, brutal, and the shame, concealed, but I could feel the wound. I could feel its gangrenous threads wrapping and twisting around her heart despite the levity in her voice, and so I just listened to her words and tried to understand what her heart needed so desperately to tell me.

Botton and Joliette had met officially in the deserts of the Sudan. Joliette was working on her doctoral thesis, and it was the first excavation of her aspiring career. As head archaeologist, Botton was in charge.

"Acceptance on the dig-team was by invitation and recommendation," she said, "and only the best and the brightest students could ever hope to be awarded such an honor. I was such a student." Joliette's invitation had come from Botton himself, which had stunned her, since they had no acquaintance — academic or otherwise — prior to that day. She had heard of him, of course, long before she had been invited to join the team. Vanity gives rise to indiscretion, and his reputation as a libertine had boldly and callously preceded him. However, true to her generous nature, Joliette was willing to put all of her preconceived notions of him aside. He was brilliant, and his passion for antiquity rivaled her own in its depth and complexity.

Under the heat of the Sudanese sun, they both reveled in the arduous toil, waiting with bated breath for the brittle landscape to give up its next treasure, and while breath came in weak spasms, it was not long before genuine friendship grew between them. A friendship borne out of a deep admiration and respect for the science, and secretly, for each other.

Upon returning to France, Joliette decided to continue her post-graduate work in Toulouse and accepted an internship with the University. Despite the cold-hearted ridicule, her research work was highly regarded, especially for someone so young, and her reputation for diligence afforded her the immense privilege of working closely with some of the greatest minds in archaeology, including Botton. Knowing this, Joliette was not the slightest bit surprised when the board requested that she accompany Botton on a high profile and heavily funded research expedition to India. It would be an expansive two-year dig, and Joliette, unkempt and manic with glee, took only a mere fortnight to gnaw her fingertips to the nub in anticipation.

As I mentioned earlier, Joliette's imagination could rival the splendor of a Greek epic, and her expectations, equally grandiose, were fulfilled the instant her feet touched the russet-colored Indian soil. The entire scale and landscape of the excavation site transcended what even she could have ever dreamt.

Situated atop a series of elaborately constructed mud-brick platforms, the ancient ruins of Lothal stand isolated and proud against the ever-shifting Sabarmati River. The site, discovered in the 1950's, was thought to be one of the most significant Harappan sites in the Indus Valley and had been, along with other sites along the coastline, under almost continuous excavation.

Joliette's preliminary research indicated that the Archaeological Survey of India had initiated the excavations of the site in 1955, and many of her own colleagues believed that this particular site was the most important center of trade between settlements in India and Western Asia. Marketplaces and trade centers had already been discovered, and the excavations brought to light the depth and sophistication of ancient urban planning and architecture. Even the less extensive surface excavations unearthed large numbers of antiquities such as seals; beads of gold, jasper, and copper; intricately carved and decorated shells; gold and silver coins; terracotta ornaments; and all manner of imaginatively decorated vessels linked to Mesopotamia, each in turn more precious than the last. The Harappan peoples here exhibited superior metalworking techniques, as well, producing tin, copper, bronze, and lead goods. The copper being the purest in the region. So pure that Botton had trouble maintaining the phlegmatic resignation his reputation had always demanded of him. In spite of his advanced years of service to the science and a temperament that had been forged from oxidized ingot, still he struggled to contain his delight.

Yes, I suppose the primitive peoples of this city could have just run naked across the lands, hitting things with sticks and being generally contented, but they hadn't. The innovative engineering skills of the Harappan peoples were remarkable and unparalleled for that particular period. They existed, and with existence there comes a million possibilities for great thought and action, for beauty, for art, and for poetry. That was what Joliette so desperately sought in the dust. She sought the idea of divinity. The driving force behind the heart and soul of man.

As Joliette stood looking out over the dock waters, she could easily imagine the city at the height of its magnificence. Vastness spread out before her, its meticulously planned shape and organization rippled into the burnt sienna for many meters. The geometry was complex, so complex that it felt instinctual. With that realization, Joliette fell to her knees, struck down by an ancient ache in her bones. Every muscle in her body felt weak, as if she were being drawn backwards into a whirlpool of time and space. She pulled her knees up to her chest and sat in silence, rocking back and forth as she listened to the water lapping against the dock. *They dug.* With all their will, they had dug in so deeply that the gods, striving to thwart their ambitions, had shifted the water beneath their feet.

The river there had risen up many times, wrapping its arms around the city and casting it in a thousand shades of silt and decay, and yet, its grandeur had neither withered nor lost itself. Battered by heat, time, and the river, this city and its peoples had once stood majestic, each crumbled brick a measure of might against the next. In the mounting heat, Joliette could almost hear the din in the streets. She could feel the tidal surge of the river, and she could smell the musky richness of the mud brick mingled seductively with a hint of human sweat and spice, rich and pungent.

A marvel of engineering the city was, but its structural artistry was not what seized Joliette's soul. You see, Lothal — mound of the dead — was so named for a reason. Its people had navigated the stars two thousand years before the Greeks. Ethereal incarnations, though mortal, they lived and breathed eternal through their art and sculpture. Death was but another journey, and their departed, in lamenting arms, were laid to rest beneath their beloved night sky. The first time Joliette excavated a joint burial and beheld the entangled bodies, the skulls resting forehead to cheek, and the slender arms extending to embrace one another, she could not help but fall victim to the phantom emotions lurking within her. She was an inconsolable wretch for three days, refusing to bathe, eat, or speak to anyone. Even then, Botton stood by her side in silence.

He was always by her side.

Despite the considerable scale of the site and the fact that their areas of expertise were quite distinct, Joliette and Botton were rarely parted from one another. The sweat drenching their burnt skin glistened like sun-kissed raindrops as the raging wind churned the sand and set it against their eyes and their spirits. Each new dawn brought fresh exhilaration and pain. Their bodies ached. The heat was unbearable, and yet, their determination never faltered. With each new discovery, no matter how small a trinket or immense a wall, they fell into embrace out of sheer joy, and much like all things endeavored upon out of true passion and love, their emotions could not and would not be contained. "In the end," Joliette confessed, "the sweltering heat and the exotic atmosphere had its intended effect. All it took was a brief reprieve to a local village, where, intoxicated on the spicy food, the equally spicy drink, and the erotic, pulsating music, we could not help but fall in love."

Joliette had a certain, shall we say, uninhibited freedom of spirit and was deeply moved by many things. Even with his mind strapped tightly to the coil, Botton had difficulty restraining his want for her. He tried to reason away his feelings, calculated the risks and the benefits, and then when he realized the variables were beyond the simple computation he sought in the dregs at the bottom of his glass, he tried to suppress them, but when the music took hold of her and the dust from the dirt floor kicked up around her bare feet in sensuous clouds of filigree and shadow, it was very difficult for him to distinguish whether she was, in fact, the serpent or the charmer.

Either way, neither could refuse one another.

Later that evening, when the earth met the sky in darkness, Joliette stood on the shoreline of the Sabarmati River. There was no wind, and a deep silence engulfed her. She felt the stillness of the land, its wrenching solitude, and even though she might have felt alone, she was never really alone. In that glistening water, the voices of the ancient people rose and fell with the current. Gasping with lament and longing, the river sent its breath rolling over the shoreline. It lingered there but for a moment to inhale a bit of the earth, and then it retreated, taking the sand and the voices with it back to the land of the dead. Often, she had wanted to follow the tide. She wanted to follow those voices — voices she had always heard so clearly in her mind — but that night, Botton stood at the shoreline with her.

He held her tight, as tightly as the moonlight, and then for no particular reason, he kissed her.

"You taste like the sand and the sea," she whispered after his lips had gently let go of hers. So faint was her voice that it seemed as if she were afraid of the words, afraid of what they meant, not to her, but what they might mean to him, and so she put her fingers to her lips to stop them revealing her secrets.

Botton just smiled, took her face in his hands, and looked into her sad, sorrowful eyes. "You taste like everything I have ever wanted," he replied.

"Don't be ridiculous, Olie…"

"Come on, Jol, don't do that. Shy doesn't suit you. No, don't pull away from me. Just look at me. It's true. You're brilliant, soulful, beautiful, charming, how the mica glitters on your skin in the moonlight, and you … you are so painfully sad. What's not to want in you? Hell, you call me Olie, and I don't hate it, but more importantly, this work you do, it's more than a career for you, Jol. It's more than a passion even. You would die to make sure the ancient voices don't."

She couldn't argue with his last statement. She would die for them. She had never been able to admit that to anyone. She pulled away from him, lowering her head to shield him from the tears, herself from the shame, and so he kissed her again, a deeply wounding kiss full of purpose and fortitude. Joliette could do little else but surrendered to it, and the moon, deaf to their words, simply cherished the moment.

For the remaining eighteen months of the excavation, Joliette and Botton's ardent exclamations would echo without hindrance throughout the encampment.

Regrettably though, as I have previously mentioned and have found to be true in this case in as much as any: All things must die. Love is no different from anything else when it comes to the existential matters of living and dying.

Botton had long ago succumbed to the demands of vanity. He was habitually foolhardy and impetuous, and his indiscretions, whether real or imagined, would not go unnoticed by my beloved Joliette. Despite the gravity of their findings, their lauded return to Toulouse was overshadowed by innuendo and rumor. Each turn of foot, as they guided her down the hallowed hallways of her academic temple, was plagued by sly glances and churlish whispers. They echoed from the very bricks that held the entire foundation of her world together.

Could it be that she was simply another conquest?

Now, if you are inclined to believe rumors, as many women are inclined to do, then the answer to that question could be nothing other than, apparently so.

It was said that Botton had an insatiable ego, and that from time to time, he would satisfy it with the best and brightest that the University had to offer. Each candidate would be hand selected with the greatest of care. He desired a woman nothing less than remarkable. He demanded intellect, beauty, and ambition. A woman highly suggestible, or more to the point — eager. This type of woman is driven by passion, and passion, Botton had discovered, was something that could be manipulated quite easily.

As a scientist, and a scholar, the idea that she had been duped bit into Joliette like a shadowy serpent, injecting its poison directly into her soul, and as that poison coursed through her veins, her disdain for Botton grew beyond the bounds of conscious restraint. She attempted to avoid him at all costs, cherished every single opportunity for rudeness without cause, and publicly belittled his romantic prowess to the best of her womanly abilities.

Nevertheless, Botton persisted for reasons unknown. Bitter and defeated, maybe he was just feeling the sting of rejection, or maybe the rawness he felt was because he had actually fallen in love with her.

Either theory would remain just that. A theory.

Time passed, and as expected, Joliette ultimately decided that she would no longer endure his torturous existence of her own free will. After only one year back at the University, she was offered an excavation of her own. She accepted without question, and she and Botton would finally go their separate ways.

4

A Theory *Borne of Will and Madness*

Kolyvan, Altai Krai — ominous, desolate, and sinister. Suitable words for this ice-bound valley of the dead, and Joliette couldn't think of anywhere else she would rather be. Here, everything was cold. Perfectly preserved and cold.

Defying the constraints of the earth, this valley lies elevated in the Altai Mountains in Siberian Russia, near the borders of China, Kazakhstan, and Mongolia. Part of the Ukok plateau, the valley is so remote that many ancient burial sites have been concealed here from all knowledge for centuries, but inevitably, what is meant to be found will be found.

Even though the tombs had been previously ransacked, looted, as well as officially excavated, Joliette's enthusiasm was not diminished at all by what she referred to as the "sloppy seconds" scenario. Her colleagues took offence at the sexual implications of the idiom, but Joliette couldn't care less what they thought. "In the early days of archaeology," she explained, "the practice of surveying a site before excavation was not common. Sites were more or less strip-mined for surface features, leaving the foundation strata greatly compromised." The term seemed to fit in this case, but she was certain that there were many equally splendid objects still to be found, objects that had escaped not only the ravages of time and thieves but had also escaped the meticulous, scrutinizing eyes of other archaeologists. A Rosetta stone, perhaps. Indeed, a find like that was certainly something to hope for, and Joliette always found hope in the earth.

Forsaking rest during the arduous trek up the mountain, her mind anxiously sorted and categorized a thousand possibilities as her heart suffered the hope of a thousand mislaid secrets. The adjustment to the punishing climate was no less intolerable, but the matter that most concerned her beyond the glacial chill that had consumed her body was the fact that other intact tombs had been found to contain remarkably well preserved human remains, and she had longed all her days to make such a monumental discovery. She knew that such a discovery could lay to waste a world of misconceptions and, for her own heart, a world of desolation, self-doubt, and disappointment.

The odds were in her favor, as it was common practice for the primitive peoples in this area, much the same as in Egypt and in the Sudan, to preserve their dead using ancient mummification techniques.

Secreted away within the jagged bowels of the mountains, the deceased — draped in sumptuous fabrics and covered with gold and jewels — were symbolically laid to rest according to the traditions dictated by their status in life. Attended to by sacrificed concubines and drawn by fleets of mummified horses, the intricately carved and elaborately ornamented coffins bore the hierarchy to the netherworld in grand style.

The ancient peoples here had spared no hardship for their dead. Despite the harshness of the landscape, the ice and cold were, in fact, an advantage in the preservation of the remains. Desiccation was always an issue, but heretical desecration proved more of a problem than the elements. Selfishness and greed are more than worthy opponents, and so the perilous location, insulated by densely forested slopes and steep rolling foothills, was a testament to the fortitude of the peoples that had once inhabited this land.

"Respect the dead as one would respect the gods," Joliette mumbled to herself, her words carried along by the wind in her hair as they reached the summit. "Build the man a tomb. Build the God a temple."

So they had.

Chiseled directly into the mountain's rock-face, the collection of temple/tombs was breathtaking, and as its magnificence unfolded through the latent shadows encircling the mountain's formidable visage, it revealed a work of artistic measure more beautiful than Joliette had ever set her eyes upon. Scarred and pitted by elemental trespass and lichen, the rough-hewn basalt and granite parapets loomed almost out of logic's reach, and the impossibly massive columns and entablatures embellishing the façades alluded to the remains of an ancient mythological Greek city. Here, at the edge of a frozen abyss, here, where the cold stopped time, Joliette had stumbled upon a mount Olympus, adorned with chariots, bleating horses, maidens a fair, and a legion of dead souls.

Joliette was convinced that the clustering of tombs in a single area like this suggested that there was a particular and extremely important ritual significance, mythological or otherwise, and one she needed to understand before her next breath was drawn. These peoples would have been willing to transport their dead over vast and treacherous distances for burial rites. Why would they risk it in the cold dry winters where the dark seemed endless or the scorching summers with little to no rain? There was no doubt in Joliette's mind that these tombs were built under the divine instruction of the gods. To suffer so for the dead defied any other logical explanation.

Even though the site had been previously excavated, Joliette felt that something else rested here. Something secret. Something missed. Something of a whisper in her ear that she could not ignore, a whisper that would eventually take possession of her very soul. A possession that would urge her forward through a year of wild emotional defeats and near-fatal injuries. A possession, obsessive and despairing, that would sustain her through the endless hours and the endless days that would pass before she, undaunted, would make her most striking discovery. One that would alter the course of her life forever. Joliette would indeed unearth a body. The mummified body of a mysteriously tattooed chieftain. And as she stared in wonderment at her find, pages and pages of exacting annotations materialized, drifted in and out of her waking thoughts, each articulation as precise as if it had already been written, but winter was upon them, and time was running out. She would have to work quickly, and quickly meant clumsy, so a thorough assessment now became a daunting task.

Deftly embalmed with peat, bark, and the greatest of care, it became apparent to her that the chieftain was once a stocky, imposing man — tall, with a powerful physique — and although much of his body had deteriorated, Joliette felt it could be safely assumed that he had died under mystifying circumstances.

Despite the vicious onslaught of time, the tattooing on the body was still clearly visible, as much as could be expected, and the desiccated flesh revealed a peculiar, interlocking sequence of designs. The body was much too elaborately decorated for a common burial rite. Joliette knew this. The uneasy chill that raked over her bones was too pronounced to ignore. She had studied thousands of burial rites. This one was unique, and now she just had to prove it.

With the precision of a surgeon, she picked over the remains as best she could. Analyzing a body *in-situ* was problematic at best. First, there was no light. The weak lumens from the floodlights seemed to soak into the walls. Secondly, the air was damp and raw, cutting at the flesh of her face, and lastly, she couldn't concentrate. Everything about the tomb left her thoughts troubled. What had once presented itself as an intriguing conundrum, she thought, had now become the painful pursuit of reason, and so Joliette had the body moved to a portable on-site laboratory where she could make her initial assessments in a well-lit, sterile environment. An environment slightly removed from the spiritual energy that had been causing her so much unease. The comforts helped, as she would spend many weeks with the body, taking photographs, jotting notes down on little scraps of paper, and talking endlessly into her voice recorder. She barely ate, she never slept, and the sweat glistening on her brow was ever present as a million absurd and irrational hypotheses slipped in and out of her conscious mind, all of them searching for even a tenuous connection.

Amidst the chaos, she noticed that there was structure to the faded images, and the overarching theme was vaguely similar to adornments noted from other cultures in the area, but she had never seen tattooed markings such as these before. Had never seen such intense and strange configurations. Metaphorical or mythological, they were too strange to disregard. The ink was driven in too deeply. Like a medieval family crest, two hideous beasts resembling dragons spread out boldly across the chest. Oxen bodies, clawed feet at the front, hooved at the back, with long twisting tails, forked tongues, and wings? Yes, wings. Leathery, but not quite those of a bat, as in the folktales of old, but they were wings, nonetheless, and the left arm bore three partially obliterated images, which Joliette could not specifically identify, though to her, they appeared to be serpents. On the front of the right leg, a line of cuneiform lettering extended from ankle clear to knee, and over the right foot, another winged creature crawled up from inside the arch, encircling the ankle with another forked tail. Forked tongues, forked tails? Joliette moved around to the other side of the table where she noticed a second confused sequence of text on the inside of the right forearm.

What did it all mean?

Linguistics study wasn't Joliette's area of expertise, and so with each enhanced image, the motif seemed further and further beyond her intellectual reach. So much of the skin had blackened or rotted away from exposure that nothing could be distinguished even under the most intense magnification. Circles, circles, and more graduating concentric circles, falling in line with the vertebral column. Tongues, tails, and a spine of circles? This was most unsettling. To Joliette, it seemed like a cryptograph of sorts. A secret incantation. Whatever it was, she would willingly sacrifice the next two years of her life attempting to decipher it ... and decipher it she did.

Preternatural instinct had always been Joliette's greatest asset, the only one she trusted in without question. She would eventually determine that the mummified man was in all probability a high priest or a temple sentry, sacrificed and emblazoned with magical incantations in order to transform man into beast, one whose spiritual conviction would shield and defend the body of a god in the afterlife.

A Guardian. A Mage.

Despite her epiphany, Joliette remained perplexed by the fact that the ritualistic depictions painted on the interior walls of the tomb indicated a secreted burial location several thousand miles away, lying at the edge of the Black Sea.

Why?

Why would they have come here to these icy mountains, and why would they have left a sentry here to watch over a vacant tomb? Why the secret, distant location, and where was the body of the God?

Troubled by the lack of empirical data to back up her conflicting assumptions, Joliette would fret over these mysteries until she drove herself to the brink of insanity.

Upon returning from Kolyvan — the emotional intensity of the excavation having quelled her resentment

— she spent some time with Botton, discussing her conclusions and exploring each and every intimate detail of her incredible theory, and as ridiculous and implausible as this theory might have seemed to Botton, dead Babylonian gods notwithstanding, her reasoning and data were sound, even if she didn't think so. He saw no cause for abandonment and humbly offered to assist in obtaining the funding that was necessary to press forward with her research.

Eighteen months later, in cooperation with the Center for Black Sea Archaeology, Joliette received the financial backing that she required, and that, along with a team of the finest archaeologists Germany had to offer, provided the means to pursue her theory.

She would leave at once, arriving in Trabzon a few hours shy of her own birthday, which she celebrated alone with a bottle of Yeni Raki and some cheese.

The small Anatolian city of Trabzon, originally founded by Greek traders in 756 BC, sits tranquil against the shoreline, cast in the windswept shadows of the Eastern Black Sea Mountains. As beautiful as it is now, at that time, it had been gasping under the strangle hold of civil war. Estranged, set in the midst of a hostile landscape — all but doomed to fire and brimstone — this city was at odds with the world around it. Despite this, it would survive mercenaries, Persian savagery, tyrannical Roman rule, and the Goths, who raped the land and burned the port to the ground. It was only later, after the fourth crusade, that the city would finally surrender itself to the Ottomans.

For Joliette, all this history was of the utmost importance in deciphering her mystery. Trabzon sat sentinel smack in the middle of the most significant migratory path on earth. So many peoples had clambered over this land, so much blood had been wed and shed that the inevitable blending of cultures obscured everything to a frustrating extent. To strictly define anything, be it a timetable or a cultural nuance, was a painful exercise in the laws of improbability.

Further complicating her endeavor was the inconvenient geography. The inland regions are unforgiving, so densely forested that nothing grows beneath the canopy but wraith and ruin. No light shines on the forest floor, and all manner of specters move effortlessly in the shadow-spell cast by the crags. Here the dilapidated monasteries and ancient burial sites are fixed directly into the sides of the mountains, as if they had been there since the birth of the mountains themselves. Much the same as in Kolyvan, one would not only require the intellectual skill of an archaeologist to evaluate and work the site, one would require the attributes of an accomplished mountain climber, as well, as the ancient tombs Joliette had her mark on were held out over a four-hundred meter vertical ascent with many treacherous irregularities to the rock.

Over time, the thin air and the lengthy, intimate forays against the mountain eventually drained Joliette of vigor. She would sustain numerous injuries over the coming months with one of many falls from the rock face delivering a significant blow to her head. Ego bruised, body bloodied, and her mind disoriented, the fall rendered her incapacitated for more than a week. The lost time consumed her, but this was minor compared to what she had endured in Kolyvan, for the mountains there defied the laws of gravity — defeated them — and

Joliette, struck with paralyzing vertigo, had lost her footing. Her pickaxe, wedged in the rock, would not release itself, and as she tugged against its will, she lost her grip and went swinging wildly by her tether only to slam back into the mountain's rock-face, sending the pickaxe into her leg. Even that hadn't stopped her. The pain was excruciating, the infection so dire she almost lost the leg, but to acknowledge it would have felt like surrender.

Joliette's desire for knowledge fueled her every quest, and should that desire crush her bones to dust, it mattered not. There was no doubt in her mind. She would eventually breach my tomb, but what she found there was not as she had ever expected.

That day, the damp had settled over the mountain in irregular layers of mist, hugging the rock and obliterating sky and sea. It was difficult to judge the relativity of anything, including one's own footing. Spatial relationships were incalculable, and so Joliette wasn't the least bit surprised that even though the tomb's façade alluded to a vertical aspect from the exterior, the interior walls slanted upwards in a pyramidal geometry. A geometry so severe and grotesque it felt alive with malice. Devoid of any relics, hieroglyphs, or ancient scripts, the murky interior chambers offered nothing to indicate that it was an actual interment site. Not a shred of evidence was to be found. A vast emptiness dominated from floor clear to ceiling, eerily featureless and foreboding. Nothing echoed its purpose, save the cold, black walls.

Confronted with such daunting ambiguity, even the most seasoned scientist's stamina would wax and wane from the effort, but my Joliette's spirit never wavered, not once, and to much ridicule, she spent endless hours crawling over the floor and walls of this tomb, looking and searching for any clue at all.

On that particular night, she had been laboring for ten hours without pause. Her hands shook. Her knees were bruised and bloodied, and her confidence, lacerated to the bone as she scrutinized every crack and indentation ad infinitum. The fact that she found anything at all was not fortune's gift, for on that night, I had aligned all of the planets just for her, rewarding her determination with the key to the universe.

Nauseous from self-doubt, exhausted by the mountain's belligerence, she might not have noticed it at all, save for the small row of cuneiform letters etched crudely into the granite floor. Letters that bore a striking resemblance to the ones tattooed to the leg of her entombed priest in Kolyvan.

Her pulse rushed. Her breath quickened.

She stood and took up her pickaxe.

In that moment, the rhythm of her heart beat wildly, its echo resonating from every corner of the chamber, and as she held the axe frozen in the air above her head, preparing herself for the first thrust of energy and motion, she closed off her mind to every wound she had sustained over the course of her life. Ironclad was her will, and her need was buried in the rock.

All she had to do was bear down.

5

Sculpting *the Face of a God*

M y Joliette would spend never-ending hours staring into the vacant hollows that had once been the windows to my soul, and even though my body was long removed from this mortal world, I could still feel her gentle touch, hear her sweet voice, and gaze upon her beautiful face. What more could one ask for in death?

It is so that when one dies their essence passes into the ether, merging with all of the other atomic particles floating throughout space and time. This is omnipresence in the purest sense of the word.

Oddly enough though, there is a good deal of superstitious nonsense one might encounter at the mere mention of photographing the dead. Say that you are going to recreate the dead person's image from rotted bones, and immediately, out come the pitchforks and torches. My Joliette had but one response to those ludicrous accusations of witchcraft. "I have no desire to steal a soul," she said once in an interview. "I shall forever humbly endeavor to give one back."

That philosophy was the fundamental nature of her life's work, her being, and her very attitude about existence. In the simplest and most poetic of terms, she believed, devoutly in her heart, that, "Even a dead thing has merit beyond this moment and essence of its existence should never fade from the world. A memory should never be cast away and forgotten as if it had meant nothing." Everything means something in a metaphysical sense, even the trivial things. At least they did to Joliette. Restoring to me my face, my name, and my honor was the least trivial of all.

Forensic facial reconstruction is the painstaking process of recreating the face of an unidentified person from their skeletal remains. To achieve this remarkable feat, a researcher must fuse together the fundamentals of art and science. Forensic science, anthropology, and anatomy to be specific. "Frankenstein might have been a mad scientist with questionable motivations," Joliette would argue, "but his logic was sound." We can bring a thing back to life. Mad Scientist? Maybe, and this was why forensic facial reconstruction was undoubtedly the most subjective and the most controversial technique practiced and discussed within the context of forensic anthropology. Yet, despite the heated debate among the deeply divided and the equally opinionated scientific minds who enjoyed debating such things, it had successfully provided evidence as to its viability and validity frequently enough that research and methodological developments continued to advance, with a determined Joliette charging ahead like a raving lunatic at the forefront of those advancements.

My old timeworn face would come to reveal itself, and so to the best of my abilities, I will now make a concerted effort to explain this remarkable process as I stood witness.

After much mental preparation, Joliette began with two-dimensional facial reconstructions, which are merely hand-drawn portraits based on radiographs, ante mortem photographs, and the skull itself. It loosened her up, she claimed. It intensified the right brain/left brain connection, to use her words, and this method would usually require the collaboration of an artist and a forensic anthropologist, but since Joliette was endowed with the talents of both disciplines, she could work in complete solitude. No small relief it was, for she preferred to work alone, as it afforded her the depth of concentration that she required to be of one unified mind. Nothing short of an apocalypse could distract her as the days passed sight unseen.

Software programs, as they are called, have been developed of late, which can quickly generate rudimentary two-dimensional images. These images can then be manipulated, allowing subtle modifications to be applied to the drawing with impressive speed and ease. Despite the obvious advantages, Joliette — an artistic purist — used the computer only to validate her mental interpretations. She chose to rely more on her intuitive sense, or her mind's eye vision of what she called the spectral image. The aura of energy left behind by the deceased.

Many of the higher-ranking archaeologists on staff did not favor Joliette's preternatural temperament. They couldn't buy in to the hocus pocus. They being the same high-ranking individuals whom had so nicknamed her gravedigger. Nevertheless, her accuracy was beyond reproach. No valid argument could be made against her methods however strange and unnatural they might have seemed to the logic-based world of science.

Tossing logic to the wind, as Joliette often did, she produced anywhere from twenty to upwards of fifty charcoal drawings of my skull in this, the initial stage of the process, adding greater and more specific detail with each successive illustration. So many there were, littering the floor, tacked to the walls, strewn across every stainless-steel work surface, that it felt like a gallery retrospective sans the caviar and elitist ambiance.

She worked with astounding precision and concentration. Rapt by the bombardment of images assaulting her mind, she seemed oblivious even to the discordant compositions screeching from her disc player. Her body swayed in tempo with a dulcet note struck far and away deep in the recesses of her subconscious mind. Every movement, every innocuous gesture, elegant by design. In a haze beset with illusion, she drifted, floated through the air like a rose petal caught in the breeze, glittering waves of charcoal dust and temperance swirling in the air around her. Magic it was. Pure magic to behold. My Joliette was nothing less than a divine conjurer.

On countless evenings, deep into the twilight hours, I could sense Botton as he stood out of sight in the dimly lit corridor, watching her, charmed and silent, smiling in the shadows. He felt something for her, felt it to the very baseless core of his existence. Reluctant to define it, the glint in his eyes betrayed his heart's desire, although his arrogance would never have allowed him to admit it. In spite of his vast intelligence, Botton was an idiot.

But alas, my amorous side can be rather disagreeable, and my mind tends to drift. We were speaking of Joliette … and my face.

The process of creating three-dimensional facial reconstructions is quite a bit more involved than a love affair gone astray. To not only define a thing, but to create it anew from scraps of rot and relic, now that takes a certain amount of stamina. The Gods were oft chiseled out of stone, sculpted from clay, or molded of precious metal. For me, modern technology would see to it that my aura could, to my astonishment, be actualized from rudimentary computer data. Transformed by a snarl of circuitry into an elaborate high-resolution three-dimensional image, the very vague, deliberately formless idea of myself could be wrenched from its eternal slumber without the slightest hint of regret.

It was all very impressive, but being an accomplished sculptor, my Joliette preferred the use of modeling clay. This method, she said, allowed her to "feel and know" the subtleties of her subject, that being a long forgotten Assyrian King. A scholar. A naive buffoon, on occasion, and lover of art and artifact.

I get ahead of myself, though. Joliette's mind was uncharted territory for me, so manic and scatterbrained she was in her thoughts that it was difficult to chart the process as exactingly as she performed it. Three steps ahead and two-fold behind, the data, empirical and theoretical, swirled about in her head as if there were no fixed axis to plot against. The modeling couldn't begin without a plaster cast, and so I was thrust into some elaborate apparatus called a CT scanner, which in turn, created a series of three-dimensional images of my skull. The skull, after all, is the foundation with which all assumptions are based. Ironically, this is true in life as well as in death.

Through careful inspection of the scans and meticulous anthropological investigation, the forensic artist can then easily approximate the thickness of the soft tissues over the skull. Additionally, any other physical evidence excavated in association with the remains would need to be taken into account, as well. Jewelry, hair, clothing, evidence of body art, all are critical to the final stages of the reconstruction because they directly affect the appearance of the individual in question.

After Joliette analyzed the CT scans a ludicrous number of times, she performed a thorough physical examination of my skull. This examination focused on identifying any abnormal pathologies or unusual landmarks such as bumps, ridges, and indentations in the bone that would deviate from the validated research data. She profiled the shape and structure of my jaw, the symmetry of the nasal bones, and my teeth, specifically the wear of the biting surfaces, as all of these features, seemingly trivial, have a profound effect on the formation and appearance of an individual's face.

Once the examination was completed, my skull was sent off to be cleaned, and then once returned to her, Joliette repaired the damaged and fragmented areas with a wax like substance. She reattached my jaw and filled the nasal openings in with clay.

At this point, a plaster cast of my skull was prepared. After the cast had set, Joliette attached to it little colored plastic markers. Twenty-one of them in all, placed at very specific areas, which corresponded to the reference data she had methodically entered into the computer over many weeks. I looked like a human pincushion, so much so that the eerie jubilation I should have been feeling was greatly diminished. All the machines. All the little dots on my face. Pins and circuits and binary data. It was so clinical. Clinical but necessary, I suppose. She had seen my face so many times in her dreams, and yet to feel my flesh, well, she hadn't stepped that far into the abyss yet, and so science must be allowed its intervention.

From this point on, Joliette would attempt to step away from her science, turn her back to the edge and look out beyond the definitive, adding all my features instinctively by hand, and this part of the process was a spectacle like no other I had ever experienced.

Bleached whiter than if my actual skull had been left out in the sun for centuries, it begged color and depth from every angle imaginable, and my Joliette would give rise to its bloom as she applied the layers of clay, thin and precise, with sublime, almost sensual strokes. It was as if a kinetic energy were surging through her grimy fingertips, channeling the paranormal force of a long lost lover. Such an eye for detail, such an adoring touch she had, I couldn't have wished for a more devoted person to revive my soul. As she spread the clay over the surface, layering the facial muscles onto the casting, Joliette's thumbs pushed in with gentle force, a force invigorated, charged with life, bringing out the masculine severity of my cheekbones, the subtle indentation in my chin, and finally, the strong sinewy curvatures of my neck.

Each individual stage in this process took weeks at a time on some occasions. Joliette was a perfectionist, and she frequently made addendums to her notes, indicating specific timetables but often mentioning that each stage would take as long as it had to. "The face, its true nature," she explained, "would find its way to the surface." All the process needed from her was a slow, steady hand.

Every detail meticulously rendered was significant, and Joliette spent no less time or attention on my nose than she had on anything else. Never having given it much thought, I was unaware that a nose is one of the most problematic features to reconstruct. Apparently just sticking it on there is the generally accepted practice, arbitrarily determined by projecting two lines from the midline of the skull. A bit slapdash for science, I thought, and Joliette would agree. The terms arbitrary and generally accepted were not found in her vocabulary, and the nose she eventually gave me was a noble nose, true and prominent, along with my lips. I fancied the thought of breathing her in. Of tasting her scent in the air.

Would that a thousand mouths lay their breath upon me.
Would that a thousand lips fancy meeting mine.
Would that I adore thee with kisses,
If only those lips were thine.

My Joliette had the most wonderful lips, ample, but not too much so, perfect in their geometry, with the soft first blush of fresh fig laid upon them, and I am quite sure they tasted as such. The desire to kiss her lips was overwhelming. A fixation I could not bear. What I would not give to experience again the rush one feels when wholly engaged by a kiss. To feel the way her body might initially resist it, and then in a rush of passion, to feel the release and the wanting that comes with it. To watch her throw herself wildly into the fury of that wanting. It is an outright injustice that most men do not appreciate the many stimulating qualities of a proper kiss. A man may, should he be so inclined, bring a woman to the very threshold of madness via the simple act of kissing. Alas, most men are not so inclined, and I do get away from myself from time to time.

With small pointed sticks and other sculpting instruments, Joliette spent painstaking hours further defining the soft tissues around my eyes, my lips, and the muscles in my face, ones that would be attributed to facial expression. Muscles that would have liked to draw a smile for her, but there was no time for sentiment. Once this was completed, my face would be fleshed. All of the tissues were then built up until the markers were completely covered, and my ears would be affixed in place. Hair, wrinkles in the skin, tattoos. In the end, six months had passed into oblivion without so much as a notice. The earth had shifted on its axis; the nights had grown cooler, the dark hours fragmented and long; and my beloved, through intense and scrupulous labor, had finally brought forth the immortal face that had been haunting her dreams for an eternity. I had been awakened. As I was. As I remember myself to be. My Joliette, my fatally flawed Joliette. For some unknown reason and against all annotated anthropological data, she had opted to give me the most spectacularly beautiful eyes. Azure. Like that of the cloudless skies rifting the ice-bejeweled mountains of my eternal homeland. It was a liberty she felt no remorse in taking. Had I the choice, it would be a reasonable assumption that I would have chosen alike, but all that mattered not. It had been so long since I had looked upon my own face, and for that, I loved her more than any creature defined by its own existence ever could. She had given me the capacity to exist again. She had given me back my immortal soul.

She gazed at me lovingly for hours that last evening,

stroking my face while whispering passionate endearments to the ether. Her hazel eyes, lustrous as sunbeams shimmering through an autumnal wood, reflected my own longing back into me.

Her ardor, though flattering, disturbed me.

Throughout the entire process, I sensed something shifting within her, and that night, her emotions, oddly beyond her control, descended upon her in torturous waves. An ancient darkness eclipsed all the light in her eyes, and she wept. Blood-soaked tears fell from her wounded soul and sank into the clay, each drop the diluted remnants of a lifetime of rage, desire, and sorrow.

The tempest lasted several hours. Breath strained and shallow, spirit mortally weakened from the long enduring struggle, Joliette, legs trembling beneath her, struggled to her feet and made her way to the lab office, where there, she collapsed into sleep on an old tattered sofa hidden off in the corner between a fortress of disordered filing cabinets. Her face, so serene in its repose, had taken on the pale surrender of death itself. It seemed as if she had given over the very last of her life's breath for me. I wished I could thank her for it, but all I could do was whisper to her soul as I gazed down upon her from the heavens, "How the grace of death suits you, my love."

Passion had ravaged her body beyond the point of exhaustion, and for a few fleeting moments, she would be free of the physical realm. As I felt her cross over into infinity's dark dominion, I knew that now was the time. A moment torn out of time where flesh and mist could become one. Alone at last, we could finally share the stolen moment that I longed for.

As she dreamt, I veiled her mind from the mortal world, veiled it with an infusion of undying ages and memories, memories flooded with velvet yearnings that would lift her up and carry her blissfully and willingly into my awaiting arms.

Upon a great steed, its mane hued of lilac and lilies, I bore her over. I bore her over the sands of time, across the many lands I had once claimed as my own. I offered her the opulence of my palace and the virtuous grandeur of my languishing heart. I read her ancient poetry from stone tablets, sweetened her palate with endless temptations, and I bed her down amidst fur, satin, and silk. I took her in her dreams that night — took her by force — a force of will and passion that I was unaware I still possessed. I made love to her. As no mortal man ever could. As no mortal man ever would.

6

Not All is Ever *as It Appears*

Botton, contemptible, stupid buffoon that he was, careered into the lab, the stack of papers taking wing from his arms as he tripped over himself and fell head-over-ass onto the floor. After a short-lived moment of humiliation, he picked himself up, leant over, and placed his hands on his knees in a somewhat comical attempt to steady himself and catch his breath, his eyes reflecting a growing state of bewilderment.

Joliette and I had been having an intense conversation on the issues of theology and errant human sexuality — no doubt brought about by the prior evening's flush of passion — and we were both quite startled by his rather flamboyant entrance, but not so startled as was he upon hearing our lurid discussion.

Mingled with heaving breaths, the words fell aimlessly from his lips as he attempted to regain some modest amount of composure. "Who in the hell are you talking to, Jol?" he asked, and Joliette paused and sighed before responding. It was then that Botton knew that composure was the least of his worries.

"The fucking dead guy, who else? Olie, you have got to stop barging in here like this. The constant interruption breaks my concentration."

"Ok, sorry, I just thought I heard voices? No matter, I received the first of the reports back," he began to explain as calmly as was possible, considering what he was about to bludgeon her with, but then he misplaced his train of thought. "Oh wow!" he continued, "Is this the guy? Rather stern looking fellow, but quite remarkable really."

"Olie!"

"I'm just teasing, Jol. He really is something, even if he does seem a little vexed."

"Olie, for fuck' sake. The reports?"

Upon recovering his original sense of direction, Botton's voice fell in tenor to a low agitated trembling. "The reports? Well, ok Jol, something is just not right, and I don't know what to make of it all yet."

"Olie, what are you talking about?"

"Well *merde*, there isn't really a simple way to explain it. The armor and the textiles, they date one thousand years later than his body does, and the sword, no one made a sword like that then. The alloy ratios are all off, some I can't identify at all, and the blade itself — no one ever folded metal like that. Not then. Not now."

"So, where is it from then?"

"You're not listening to me, Jol. No One made a sword like that. Not then, not now, not ever."

"Are you sure?" Her sarcasm implied she was certain that he was having a bit of a laugh at her expense.

He was not.

"Positive. I have been over the data five times already. There's no question."

Joliette felt a faint icy tingling sensation in her fingers. Her face exploded in a flush of heat, and her knees weakened. She grabbed hold of the table to steady herself, and so Botton leant in to her and lifted her chin to get a better look at her face. When he did, his brow furrowed slightly, and his feigned concern nauseated me. "You don't look well, Jol." He grabbed her shoulders and guided her towards a waiting stool. "You have barely left the lab in months," he added. "How much sleep have you had lately?"

"I'm fine," she responded firmly. "I just have a headache, that's all. I need to look at that data." She snatched at the documents still clenched in his arms, and he recoiled defensively, prompting her to scold him, "Olivier, don't be a child."

Botton gave a weighty groan in defeat and surrendered the papers over to her. Subsequently, they both set about gathering the remainder from the floor. Once all of the various documents had been laid out systematically, Joliette put on her glasses. She and Botton were in for an arduous afternoon.

The sheer quantity of data Botton had amassed was overwhelming. Charts, graphs, and reams of statistical data obtained from the various methodologies he had used, including, but not limited to X-ray fluorescence; inductively coupled plasma mass spectrometry; laser induced breakdown spectroscopy; neutron activation analysis; lead, strontium, and oxygen isotope analysis; potassium-argon dating; radiocarbon dating, and an even longer list of more befuddling acronyms I don't care to expound upon.

With regret, all I could do was watch with an imagined stifled breath as they tried to wrap their minds around the enigma they had been presented with.

Eight hours passed, some in silence, some with disconcerted stares and the nervous pacing of floors, and some with the apropos colorful language indicative of utter frustration. Joliette had reached the threshold of her endurance. The bottom had dropped out of her world. All her assumptions were now in question, all her certainties were now uncertain. She sat slumped over the lab table, glasses hanging precariously from her ear as she massaged her temples in vain. The pain and confusion was obvious. Her eyes hurt so intensely that the pages had become nothing more than a smear of despair.

Botton was in much the same state. Equally exhausted, his patience strained to its limit, he looked a man awaiting his own execution, with a dull axe and a farsighted executioner, no less. Elbows resting upon his knees, fingers entangled in his hair, he sat on the sofa in the office across the room from her. It took all of the energy remaining in his body to rouse himself from his mental stupor, lift his head, and make the declaration that they should cease and desist, well, at least for a moment anyway. "Jol, come on," he shouted to her from the sofa. "Let's get out of here for a while. My place. I'll cook … and I'll keep my hands in my pockets. I promise."

Among other things, Botton was also a liar.

7

The Passion *of a Woman, the Treachery of a Man*

L ater that night, Joliette came to me in a ragged
state. I felt in her a sadness so infinite, so hollow
that she could do little but surrender to it, and
that surrender caused the heart of my soul to break open.
The denial, less fragile than her emotions, fell from her
lips, brash and firm, through the flood of tears as she
paced the cold tiled floor of the lab.

"I don't know what I am doing," she cried out. "I
don't know how I am supposed to feel, or even if I can
feel anything anymore, and yet, I ache.

"Lonely — No!" she declared as she slammed her
purse down onto the desk in the office, scattering its
worthless contents about the room. Then, when she
realized that she still had her stockings clenched tightly in
her hand, she looked at them in disgust, wadded them up
into a ball, flung them across the room, and then
proceeded to plummet barefoot towards the sofa, as if she

had lead weights tied around her neck. "I am not lonely," she continued as she curled herself up into the cushions, knees pressed tightly to her chest. "Damn it. I live a solitary life, and I like it that way. Solitude is not lonely. It's close…" She squeezed her legs tighter and rested her forehead against her knees as she continued in a weak, broken whisper, "It's just close … but its walls are strong," she added, "strong, yet moss covered and soft, just like the ancient temples, comforting in the way that they are overflowing with long lost memories. Memories that know only you, know the substance of your soul. That's how it is. Not lonely."

As her voice trailed off, it became clear to me that she was trying to convince herself of something, or maybe deny herself something. Savage primitive background duly noted, even I understand that every woman has needs just as great as a man's, and a woman who felt as deeply to her soul as my Joliette had needs even greater than that. Botton had a way with the mechanics of love and desire. Considering his good looks and his overt and charismatic demeanor, he was obviously afforded much practice in that arena. It was not surprising that she would succumb to his wiles, and my heart bled for her as she recounted the evening.

But I saw the truth.

Joliette had agreed to have dinner with Botton at his home that very evening, as his invitation had been received as harmless, albeit under the guise of going over the data. Joliette desperately needed the distraction, and Botton intended to take full advantage of her disordered mental state. He would ply his charms with absolute mastery. My beloved could never have resisted, her weakened heart was no match for his trickery.

Botton's residence was a three-story brick home overlooking the Canal du Midi. It was amply ornamented and swathed in warm, earthy hues. Lush textiles and vivid tapestries hung from the walls, complimenting the opulent fabrics of the furniture and the window dressings. The walls were littered with ancient weapons — antique and replica alike — intermingled with dozens of photographs in gilded frames depicting the many archaeological excavations from the late 1920's to present day. Hundreds of sepia-tinted faces stared out, smiling, wide-eyed, as they gloated over the spoils.

All this bric-a-brac, useless relics really, but to Botton, his collection was a tangible testament to a life — his life — lavish and comfortable, though reeking of self-importance. For a youngish man, he was rooted much too deeply, and this overabundant display of means stood in sharp contrast to Joliette's diminutive, stark, studio sublet. Sparsely furnished, cluttered with scientific papers, sterile, practical, and rarely occupied, yet, she felt quite at ease in Botton's home. This, I imagine, was mostly due to the fact that Botton lived and loved everything about who he was. His entire presence was evocative of quicksand — suffocating in pretentiousness — and there was no use struggling against it.

Her hesitant step across the threshold confirmed that she was entirely at his mercy, and he had set the snare splendidly. Candlelight during dinner, a bottle of his oldest and finest vintage, the sultry breeze blowing in from the canal. Yes, the illusion was perfection.

During the meal, they sat at a long antique mahogany dining table, Joliette at the head of the table, Botton seated right next to her. The crystal wineglasses shimmered in the candlelight, and they sat and ate in silence, both too exhausted to articulate clearly on any of the theories tumbling wildly through their heads.

Every now and then, Botton would reach out to touch Joliette's hand and say something to her, something witty or poetic perhaps, but when she looked up from her plate at him, his words choked in his throat, and he had to grab for his wine glass and swallow hard. The situation was no more comfortable for Joliette, she simply had a better command of her manners, and so she arose from her chair, and in an effort to put an end to the ridiculous charade, she offered Botton a bit of well-meaning flattery as she took up the plates and proceeded to clear them from the room. "I had forgotten what an outstanding chef you are," she said.

"Just one of my many humble talents," he boasted in jest with an equally awkward grin as he got up and followed her into the kitchen. He set the cutlery down on the counter, retrieved a bottle wine from the chiller, and nonchalantly uncorked it and poured himself another glass.

'Yes, humble of course,' she thought in between idle sips of tap water as she attempted to make a mental note of how much exactly she and Botton had had to drink, but she'd lost count somewhere during the hors d ' oeuvre course. That was dangerous. He knew all her weaknesses, but that confession was best left unsaid, and so she tried to recover with a comedic departure from the subject at hand, "What's a sure way to pacify an archaeologist?"

Botton gave an accidental snort and spat his wine into the air. "Give them bones to eat," he shouted in reply. "I can't believe you remembered that. Ha, what did you say, Jol? 'They'll be at it for hours if you give them a crab fork.' I've never seen director Henri speechless until that night."

As Botton's voice bellowed out with an unfettered jubilance, my Joliette could not help herself. She covered her mouth lightly with her fingers and sent a laugh aloft into the anxious air. A smooth, luxurious laugh that could light up the darkest of tombs. Her spirit rang out clearly through her laugh, bold, yet alluring, with a touch of shyness. There was no artifice in it, and Botton could not help but smile back in appreciation while he wiped the dripping wine from his face.

But Joliette could sense something more than appreciation in that smile, so she skirted by him, returned to the dining table, closed her eyes as if making a wish, and gently blew the candles out. She took up her own wine glass and then walked through the living room out onto the balcony. The night air was gentle and warm, infused with the scent of jasmine as the moonlight played softly off the thousand brilliant white flowers cascading over the trellis. Joliette took a sip of her wine, and while gazing up into the starlit sky for comfort, she mused aloud to herself, "Six months in the lab and how I long for the wide open sky with every fiber of my being. That moon, it calls to me. It knows me so well, and I want to answer, but when I am away from this place, I surely do miss this city."

Botton came up upon her in silence and embraced her tenderly from behind. He closed his eyes and rested his chin on her shoulder. "The city misses you as well," he whispered in reply as he took in the perfume of her hair, but Joliette refused to acknowledge the intimacy, and yet again, she managed to work her way free of his embrace. She made her way back to the sofa, where after grabbing a fistful of papers from the side-table, she sat down in a fit of frustration.

"None of this makes any sense, Olie. I don't even know what the fuck I am looking at!" She flung her arms out wide, casting the papers into the air with reckless disregard.

"Jol — please," he hollered from the balcony as he stared out over the canal in an effort to steel his nerves for the coming argument. "We have been poring over that for hours now. You need to take a break. We both need to take a break."

"Don't tell me what I need, Olie. What I need is a Rosetta stone, but I'd settle for a cheap plastic decoder ring. This data is impossible, purely and simply impossible. We will have to run all of the tests again and again after that if it still doesn't make any sense."

"I know, Jol, and I will do that, but not tonight."

He sat down next to her, offering her a genuine look of concern. She didn't buy it. "Don't you get it, Olie? If this turns sour, I'll be standing up there like one o'clock half struck. I will look like a fucking idiot." She bowed her head in defeat and continued solemnly, "My career will be over — over as in dead and fit to be buried in one of those old tombs."

"For Christ's sake. What is wrong with you, Jol? We have had mysterious results before, so what." He brushed the fall of hair from her shoulder so that he might caress the back of her neck. "What's really wrong now? Your hands are frigid, your neck feels like a piece of rope, and I have never seen you quite this manic."

Joliette closed her eyes and leant into his caresses.

"It's these goddamn headaches, Olie, I can't think straight. Something about this one ... I don't know." Botton grabbed her hand and began kneading the mound of flesh enclosing the joint of her thumb. She let out an abrupt sigh of relief, took a large sip of wine as if it were nothing more than water, closed her eyes again, and sank back into the cushions. "You always know how to get rid of my headaches."

"Ah — just another one of those…"

"Humble talents," said Joliette, finishing his sentence as she swooned with relief, and so Botton continued massaging her hand with a rather odd mix of emotion, of which its complexity, I am certain, evaded even his superior analytical mind at that moment.

"We will figure it out, Jol. You're beyond brilliant, and I am a talented hack, and between the two of us, we will figure this out, ok?"

The mild self-deprecation and his soft tone placated her nerves for a moment, a moment just long enough to regret away a secret into the warm breeze. "It's just that … I know who he is, Olie. Somehow … I don't know. I can feel him … somewhere deep in my mind."

Botton had always been, not the least bit skeptical, but more intimidated by her alleged sixth-sense, and it sent cold shivers coursing down his spine — a most unpleasant feeling — which he brushed off with a ridiculously contrived idea. "I know," Botton exclaimed as he leapt up from the sofa. "I have just the thing to take our minds off of this." He hurried to the stereo and placed a disc in the player. Within a minute or so, the dulcet tones of a sitar fused with an erotic mélange of percussion filled the room. Botton moved back over to Joliette, and with a sly grin fixed upon his face, he held out his hand with little regard. "Dance with me, Jol."

"No, no, no, Olie, I have had way too much to drink."

"Come on, Jol. You need to lighten up, just a little. I'm in my socks, utterly defenseless, and anyway, it's been two years, and until I passed by the lab on my way out the other night, I had almost forgotten how much you like this music."

"For fuck' sake, were you spying on me?"

"No, of course not. I heard the music, that's all. It reminded me of how much I used to love watching you dance. Then, there you were — dancing — right there in the lab — dancing for the dead guy. I thought it funny at first, but then, I could not take my eyes off you. Please, Jol. For old time's sake ... like when we were in India."

His plea was skillful, full of obvious deceit, and even though Joliette was not taken in by the ruse, she exhaled a leaden sigh of surrender anyway, mumbling under her breath as she reluctantly took his hand, "And we all know exactly how that turned out, don't we?"

Botton knew. He smiled, spun her about, and pulled her in close, pressing his body firmly to hers.

Casting a warm swell of ecstasy over them, the music instantly drew them in, and what two years' time had attempted to erase, and their minds had tried desperately to forget, their bodies could not help but remember.

Joliette remembered the wet of his lips, slick with anticipation and the heat of his trembling breath, and he remembered how she tasted, the velvety softness of her hands against his flesh, and the intoxicating way that the music moved through her.

All the complications of the world vanished as they swayed to the rhythm of those long misplaced memories. A wicked rhythm. Uncoiling out of the darkness, it held them captive as their bodies and minds recalled the desperate passion that they had once felt for one another. In that moment, a maudlin Joliette, having lost all measure of rational sensibility, looked deeply into

Botton's eyes and asked the only question that she truly desired the answer to, the only question that she already knew the answer to, and the answer to which, would have made no difference, "Are you going to seduce me now?"

To which he replied, "Of course."

It seemed an eternity since Botton had felt the heat of her flesh against his, and amidst the garish tapestries, the muted lighting, and the silky soft linen of his bed, he bestowing a shower of tender caresses and kisses upon her. She allowed him that, and for the moment, he felt satisfied, so satisfied that for once, he could feel her trembling at his touch, and despite all of the trite compulsions, it still made him feel like the man he wanted to be, maybe even the man she wanted him to be. All the things he had been unable to say to her, share with her, now seemed possible. The pent-up emotions. The empty years. The long-restrained desire. Yes, infinite were the possibilities, tearing at his heart and his soul. The love he felt for her, lying as a temperate dew upon his flesh, seemed but a gentle word away, but the shadowy air encircling her refused to abandon its armored grasp. His motivations would be forever doomed to remain silent and superficial.

When her face met with his, he tilted his head back and looked her in the eyes. A gentle, needful look he received back in reply, and so he dug his hands into her hair and then kissed her softly. It had been so long since he had looked up into her face like this, since her kisses had grazed his lips like whispered secrets, since he had felt the loose tangles of her hair falling seductively against his skin. The thrust of her hips. The throw of her shoulder. The perfume faintly scenting her wrists. He could scarcely bear the thought of her, the taste of her, and once again, he was laid to waste in awe of her, in awe of how she could so easily express her own need, how she could just give herself over completely to a moment, and in that moment, he felt innocent, as if she had forgiven him all his sins.

To my amazement, the innocence was genuine. Botton did not want the moment to end. He wanted nothing more than to relinquish his fear and embrace the abandon that he felt when he was with her, but he also felt oddly powerless — his fortitude a mere shadow of her might. So as always, he was more than happy to accommodate her desires while forsaking his own. Joliette took what she needed of him, while he wept quietly in the dark.

Subsequent to the many exquisitely satisfying hours of love-making, a gentle stillness flowed in to surround them, and Joliette finally managed to sleep for a few hours before awakening, severely agitated by a state of panic that had come out of nowhere to assail her. The erotic, alcohol-induced euphoria having all but evaporated, she felt nothing but a terror-fueled hysteria, washing over the whole of her body in a crest of numbing waves. She stumbled out of the bed, waking Botton in the process. "Oh Jol, not again," he said as he attempted to clear his throat and his mind.

"I have to go, Olie!"

"It's two in the morning, Jol."

Snatching her underwear up hastily from the floor, Joliette realized she had no reason for leaving aside from the cynical justifications streaking through her mind. She had no reply either other than a flat-out lie, which tumbled from her lips with little consideration. She had thought of something, and she did have to get back to the lab straight away, but Botton wasn't buying it. He scrambled towards the edge of the bed, wrapping the bed sheets around his body in some feeble attempt at humility. "Jol — come on. Please stay. I want you to stay," he offered, but her rejection, barely whispered, came quick as she stumbled over herself in a befuddled attempt to put on her stockings and shoes. "I miss you," he continued with persistence, "Please."

"Stop it," she replied, "Just shut up now, Olie. The sincerity is ineffective … and don't beg, it's beneath you."

"Jol?"

"No, Olie, You are going to ruin everything."

"Come on, Jol, I want to work this out. I want to be what you need. I just don't know how."

"What kind of fucked up thing is that to say? I don't want you to be anything. I don't have some abstract idea … don't look at me with that patronizing expression on your face … you know what I am talking about. I want you to be honest. That's all I want. Why can't you just say it?"

"Please, Jol."

"Look … I don't want to go, I don't want to stay, and I don't want to continue with this stale conversation, either. When I wanted you and me, you wanted something else … others … I don't know. What more can I say? I will see you tomorrow. I had a lovely time, really. I just … I just have to go now." She grabbed her jacket and the rest of her clothing and then hurried from the room.

Upon the hollow slam of the front door, the room closed in around Botton. The thin shadows seemed to mock his pain, and a look of inexpressible grief overspread his face. He flung himself onto his back, grabbed his hair, and even though he had half a mind to scream aloud, he uttered not a sound.

I was not quite certain how I felt for him, or how I should have felt for him, but I think I did actually feel something.

Would Joliette have stayed if she had witnessed his pain as I had witnessed it? Who can say for certain? I might venture a guess, but, even if I had such an answer, my view on the matter could do little to ease Botton's suffering. For in his vanity, you see, he actually believed that the situation was entirely about him, about something that he had or had not done maybe, or, it might possibly have been something lacking in his performance. Although he knew that was unlikely, but all considerations had to be taken into account, nonetheless. In any case, what Botton had not accounted for was the fact that Joliette had been listening to that music long before their trip to India.

It wasn't her favorite music. It was that of another, and once upon a time, she had given herself over to that music every night, the endless passionate nights on which she had danced for him.

Botton had met his match — in a ghost.

And, yes. I did, in fact, pity him.

Who is this that comes towards me out of the smoke in the wilderness; how beautiful you are my love. Thy lips are like a crimson thread, and thy mouth is lovely. Thou art all fair my love, and there is no flaw in you.

—Song of Solomon

8

A **Brief** *Intermission*

A woman's first love is, by its very nature, a rather dubious state of affairs and one against which she will measure all of the other romantic encounters in her life. Long after that first love had faded away to memory, she would have idealized it, reinvented it, then molded it and refashioned it into a first-rate mythology — a fairy tale, if you will — where all princes are handsome to the point of cruelty, are senselessly forthright and just, not to mention that they are sexually and emotionally adept to ridiculous inhuman proportions. Consequently, all princesses live happily ever after in the throes of wild, stupefying orgasms while swooning at equally wild and stupefying poetic words. Yes, a fairy tale that would be, one that no mortal man could ever possibly hope to live up to.

For my beautiful Joliette, a chance encounter with a stranger would alter her fairy tale ideal forever.

It was a fine grey London day in the borough of Harrow. Joliette, still reeling from her twentieth birthday party — now two weeks passed — had decided to spend the day shopping in London city proper with her friends. You see, this might have been her last year of freedom before returning to academia, as her family was no doubt at their wits' end regarding her decision to take a break before returning to school. She had not planned on the break being so lengthy, but an unadulterated sense of abandon had taken hold of her, and she wanted to live just a little. A little reckless. A little tongue-in-cheek. A lot unrestrained by the expectations of others. There was time enough for expectations and all the disappointments that accompany them, but that time was not now, not for Joliette.

It had been a lovely day, a day of tickled fancies and girlish twittering, with lots of window shopping, lots of bloke watching, and maybe one too many pints at the pub. At the station, she sighed heavily in the direction of the cold and distant ticket clerk, paid her fare, boarded the train destined for home, and then chose a seat close to the exit. Actually, she had had her pick of seats. The train was empty, serenely so, which was not surprising at that off-hour of the afternoon, and Joliette sat by the window, finding the silence a bit tedious though comforting. A nice relaxing ride home it would be then, she thought as the memories of the afternoon swirled about frivolously in her head. Nice enough for a bit of light reading and maybe even nice enough for a naughty daydream or two. But just when Joliette had resigned her thoughts, assuming that the remainder of the day would melt away into banality, a soft voice caught her ear, "What are you reading?"

Ever so slightly startled, Joliette shook herself back into the present. "I beg your pardon?" she asked as she turned to seek out her inquisitor, finding the man seated opposite her quite different in appearance from what she had initially imagined from his voice.

"I'm sorry," he said with an almost ludicrous air of decorum. "That was rather abrupt of me. I was simply inquiring as to what it was that you were reading." He pointed to the book in her lap. "I didn't mean to wake you."

"No, you didn't … I wasn't … Oscar Wilde," she replied after clutching the paperback to her chest. "I'm reading Oscar Wilde."

He nodded and smiled with closed and restrained lips, and Joliette felt a sudden blast of heat hit her in the face. She cleared her throat and shifted nervously in her seat. Well, maybe not nervously. It was actually more of a flush that had overcome my Joliette, as the strange inquisitor with the unnatural poetic softness to his voice was the most oddly handsome fellow she had ever set her eyes upon.

Sensing her curiosity, he opted to continue the conversation directly. "Is there something that you like about Wilde in particular?"

"No," she lied as a twinge of shyness sent her eyes to the floor, "not in particular. I just fancy a good story. It gives the mind a little holiday from the dullness of London. I am sure you can appreciate that, proper suit and all."

"Ah yes," he declared with a less reserved smile than he had previously bandied about. "Illusion is the first of all pleasures. Wilde said that, you know."

Fascinated and equally intrigued by thoughts of

unspoken intentions, Joliette somehow managed to pry her eyes from her shoes, look over at him, and smile in return. "Yes, I knew that," she replied.

Intentions aside, his eyes could not have been more mysterious. Sparkling, yet as misty grey and impenetrable as that of the skies of London. Joliette could not help herself, as her curiosity was much more than she could bear. "What's your name?" she asked with a sumptuous almost dreamy inflection.

"Fletcher and yours?"

"Joliette."

"It's lovely to make your acquaintance, Joliette." He unbuttoned his overcoat, ran his fingers down the length of his tie, crossed his left leg over his right, and then placed his hands upon his knee.

Subtle was the invitation, and Joliette found herself hard-pressed to decline. She had traveled this very route a million times in her life it seemed, and yet, as the train rattled and clanked along its tracks, she could not recall a single train ride before this one. Her mind had gone blank. She might have, in her state of delirium, even forgotten her name. She had often guffawed at the idea of mesmerism and hypnotism. It wasn't that she didn't want to believe in it. She did. It was just that she was too strong willed to let the wool get all tangled up in her eyelashes, but at that moment, looking into his eyes, she felt conquered, defeated by his every word and gesture, and so she suddenly changed her mind.

Fletcher had a seductive easiness about him, and the conversation was light and airy. Not about mundane things like the shite London weather or who was fit to have the piss taken out of them for what, but a truly meaningful conversation, a mutual discourse about art and literature and how a simple word could make you feel its breath.

My Joliette was a true poetic soul, and for the first time in her life, she felt an inexplicable tightness in her chest. She did not wish to be parted from her fine mannered stranger, but the train was coming up on Harrow /Wealdstone. The thought of inviting him home did cross her mind, but it was a fleeting thought, as her Aunt and Uncle would not have appreciated their randy niece picking up a stray bloke from the train. To say the least, they would have been mortified, all silent and scowling.

"This is my stop," she announced with a hint of disappointment as the station came into view.

"Yes, I suppose it is then," he replied in kind.

As the train slowed to its stop, she placed the Oscar Wilde on his lap. "Take this," she said, and then, in a fit of unrepressed girlishness, she leant in, quickly kissed him on the lips, and then hurried from the train.

Standing on the platform, frozen in the bleak churn of time, her thoughts darkened as the train sped past her and away. She felt his eyes upon her, knew that he was watching her from the window, but she didn't — couldn't — look back.

The long walk home was lonely and cold that day, worried by notions of what might have been, and as the sky clung desperate to the grey, his name echoed in her thoughts. Fletcher. Settling into her soul, the sky felt oppressive. The pavement, cruel under her feet, and the wind's bite felt a little deeper, deeper than she could ever remember. It chilled her through, and no amount of rationalization could ease away the tension in her heart.

Despite her best efforts to distract herself, his face and

his voice haunted her every dream that evening — heated, anxious dreams of bodies entangled, moving to the sublime rhythm of some ethereal, poetic syntax — and I felt a touch of warmth at this, her most innocent of memories. Splendid are the desires of youth, the flush of which has no rival.

The very next afternoon, the doorbell rang, and to Joliette's disbelief, there stood Fletcher, clean-shaven with a very mannerly and uncomplicated grin on his face. He was shorter than she had assumed, although her assumptions were a bit misguided, since she had only seen him seated on the train. Slight of build and rather spruce in his olive-colored suit and russet loafers, he was reasonably handsome, in a vaudevillian sort of way, with wavy, short-cropped, chestnut colored hair, full lips, and a clever, yet disarming smile.

"Hello there, Joliette. It is a delight to see you again, and I do so hope that you will pardon this dreadful, unsolicited intrusion. I am normally more well-mannered than this. I would have announced myself, but I did not have your number. I believe you misplaced this on the train yesterday." He smiled in a way that seemed to her like an apology as he held out her wallet and a small mangled spray of wilting wildflowers.

"Thank you," she muttered with a bit of chop in her voice, "I wasn't aware that I had misplaced it."

"Well then," he replied, "That's very fine, indeed. I shall count this as my good turn for the day. Would you, by chance, like to come into town with me for tea?"

Joliette, still in shock, turning the wallet over and over in her hands, had no suitable reply, and it was of little consequence, as none was actually needed.

So after another overly-romanticized train ride, they

found a quaint little outdoor café, out of the way of the hustle and bustle of London center. Joliette placed the raggedy flowers in her glass of water, and then, speaking as if they had known one another in a prior life, the conversation flowed forth with an effortless almost elegant intimacy. They spoke of all things inspiring, including Fletcher's insatiable passion for roadside weeds and poetry. Chickweed to chicory and Rilke full circle to Rimbaud, he was quite astute and understood a thing or two about the depth and breadth of the written word, and his great enthusiasm for it illuminated his face.

Joliette, being quite astute herself, was completely captivated by his discourse, but not so much so that she would ignore the sense of intrigue that tugged at her mind. She covertly shifted the conversation to satisfy her curiosity. "So, why is it that you came to my home today? To return a lost wallet, you say, is that correct? You know, you could have turned it in at the station, or with the local police."

"In truth," he replied, "the wallet was a lucky find. I actually wanted to see you again."

"So you say you found my wallet then?"

"Yes? Yes, of course. I did find it … on the train."

"Interesting," she said without even acknowledging the hint of confusion she had picked up in his voice, without even so much as a tremor in her will, and then with the utmost candor, she leant forward, looked him directly in the eyes, and then asked, "If I might be so bold…?"

"Please," he replied, "by all means, do go on."

"Well, Fletcher, if that is your real name, I think that you stole my wallet in order to gain some advantage."

Fletcher sat back hard in his seat, crossed his arms

over his chest. Her boldness had struck the loose-fitting grin from his face, and now there was much more than a glimmer in his eye. "And what makes you say that?"

"Please, I'm not daft, at least show me that courtesy," proclaimed Joliette with an unmatched pretentiousness and a furtive smile, and his parry came with equal confidence and resolve.

"And what is it, pray tell, that you have distinguished about me then?"

"Thank you for asking. First…," She patted her lips with the napkin, set it down on the table, and locked her fingers around her cup of tea. "I am quite skilled in the art of interpretation, you see. I can distinguish many things from the subtleties of a person's facial expressions and mannerisms. Things they wish to hide. I sense that this man before me, this Fletcher, might very well be a thief … but he certainly isn't a liar."

Joliette lingered at her cup of tea for a minute in order to give him a chance to recover. She could tell by the wideness of his eyes, the stiffness in his shoulders, and the hint of perspiration on his upper lip that her answer had caught him by surprise, but the loaded response that leapt off his lips without pause caught her equally so. "I think I love you," said Fletcher with the full force of his will.

Two hundred cigarettes and a half a dozen cups of tea later, they ended up back at his flat, which was shot off a dark, dank alley street, hidden in a rather seedy part of London — a part not worth mentioning, let alone living there — but Joliette had never felt safer in her life. For a rehabilitated depot, shoddy façade aside, the interior space was unexpectedly well equipped and crisp. The flat, art deco minimalist by design, was as sharp and well-tailored as the suits Fletcher wore, though it was surprising that Joliette even had a look at the place. Shortly after stumbling through the front door, they fell upon one another in a wild outburst of innocent fumbling giddiness. Their clothes, mingled with wildflower pollen and petals, wound up strewn about the entire flat.

Now, if anyone should tell you otherwise, they are lying. Size does matter, and all things are relative to that simple and oftentimes ignorantly overlooked truth. I am not speaking of the size of one's own endowments, so don't be daft, as my Joliette would say. I am speaking of the size of a man's spirit, the manner in which he carries himself. A man needs to know how to handle himself. Self-confidence, diplomacy, and the ability count for everything when it comes to pleasing a woman, especially a woman of my Joliette's particularly concentrated disposition. A man must know his worth, and Fletcher's was larger than life. He had been favored with an intensely savage array of emotions, and the eloquent manner with which he dispensed with them was an enviable talent. He was poetic, charming, dangerous, and he had a zest for life that bordered on suicidal. He may have been lacking in stature, but he more than made up for that shortcoming in all of the other areas that mattered most to Joliette. In an instant, he had come face to face with his heart's desire, and he knew it.

Joliette's recklessness on that day had been an exhilarating revelation and an enticement that self-discipline and academic sensibility could not dispute or deny. For the first time in her life, she felt accepted, adored. She finally felt connected in some small way to a forbidden self, free to express the darkest depths of her heart and her soul without feeling ashamed of her intelligence or her desires, and so she and Fletcher made love for hours on end that day, pausing only to recover their breath. "So, what do you do for a living?" she asked with a winded tremor as she pursed her lips and lit up a cigarette for the both of them.

"I'm a thieving bastard. Isn't that what you implied during our last conversation? You probably think I stole the flowers too." Fletcher wasn't lying, nor was he being purposefully flippant, for he was an honest man. "Oh come on," he continued, his tone tempered a bit. "Stop looking at me like that. I didn't steal the flowers, and even if I had, so what. Yes, I can hustle a few quid here and there, for certain, but the term bastard might be a bit too harsh. In fact, I suppose I am a thief, more or less. Never labeled myself as such. Labels seem so extreme. Too extreme for a bit of card sharking, a bit of weed peddling, and a bit of money laundering, but mostly, I just put the right people in touch with the wrong people. No, I'm not a mercenary. I make a lot of money … a lot of money for a lot of people — interesting, entrepreneurial type people, like myself — but I've never, never once, bloodied my hands. Never once even considered it, but enough about me, what about you?" he asked after taking the cigarette and promptly exhaling a ring of smoke as indifferently as he had just confessed. "What do you do? I'm sure it isn't as film noir as all that."

"No, it's nothing even remotely that stylish," she agreed. "Actually, at this exact moment, I do nothing, pretty much a whole lot of idle nothing, though I am planning on returning to university, sooner or later. I just want to experience a little bit of the world first. I want to know what it is that's so damn exciting about being young and impetuous."

"And how's that working out for you then?" He smiled, all things considered, and she smiled back.

"Right now? Bloody brilliant, I suppose. Yes, brilliant, that's how things are working out for me. If I do say so myself."

"So…," Fletcher asked, exhaling another loose tendril of smoke as he handed her the cigarette. "Brilliant idle shit aside, what do you want to do then?"

Joliette took the cigarette, rolled over onto her back, and stared at the ceiling in a desperate attempt to find the right words before answering, but all that came out of her mouth besides the smoke was, "I want to dig up dead things."

Fletcher coughed and expectedly looked at her a bit confused. "What? Dig 'em up and do what? Then what? I don't get it. Why? You mean like some sort of H.P. Lovecraft reanimator thing?"

"Yes, something like that," she confirmed through a hesitant little giggle, and Fletcher just smiled, holding back the urge to fall over himself in hysterical laughter.

"Well, now," he said, "that is something. Unexpected, yes, but something." He pulled her in close and began kissing her feverishly through his words, "You, Joliette…" A kiss to her nose, a kiss to her cheek. "You are definitely something." A kiss to her left breast, then kisses the length of her, all the way down to her feet. "What do your parents think about all that?"

"They're not my parents. Aunt and Uncle, actually. I think you might have missed a spot, yes, right there, but seriously, I was born in France, raised in the States, was thirteen when I came here."

"That explains a few things."

"I know. People notice the crap accent sometimes,

and the arrogance. They say I'm a bit off. I suppose that means I'm affected then. Isn't that what it's called?"

"Maybe. I don't know. Who isn't a bit off, but that doesn't mean it matters, now does it?"

"Not much has mattered to me in a long time."

"That's a cynical thing to say to someone you just met. It comes dangerously close to serious intimacy."

"Yes well, we are naked, in case you hadn't noticed, and some of the things we just did I'm sure are illegal, so I think we have crossed that line and then some, but I'm equally sure it's far less offensive than the things that could be said about a young woman, like myself, shagging someone she just met. If I'm a smidgen cynical, it's only because it suits me."

"I don't think cynical suits anyone, unless you're a villain, and most of them really are just sarcastic."

Joliette smiled. She wanted to cry, but the tenderness of his lips against her skin released her in some way, and she just smiled. The conversation had taken a turn, and she could appreciate his unease at its tenor, so she returned the gesture. "By your admission, it takes a villain to know a villain, but it's not that. I suppose I just got sad one day. I don't want to dump anything on you, but you see, I know for a fact that certain moments in life just have of a way of attaching themselves to you. Sometimes by way of a head-on collision. Doesn't take much … a slick road, the street lights flickering in the rain, every reflective surface mirroring nothing but the darkness, and the hundred year old gnarled tree just sitting there unyielding at the edge of obscurity. You survive, but somehow the ice and cold get driven into your heart, and an ocean of time with the wind at your back won't do anything to change it. Eventually, life just slips off into the periphery."

"I'm sorry, Joliette."

"So am I, but we all suffer tragedy. Doesn't make anyone special, so no worries, and sometimes ... sometimes we just lose a wallet, right?"

"Or find one."

An hour or so later, spent from the lovemaking, Joliette lay disheveled amidst a chaos of sheets, soaked in the last desperate breaths of their passion. In the dim florescence of the street lamp filtered through the dirty window, she gazed at Fletcher — her sleeping stranger — her poetic, thieving bastard — and in that single moment of clarity, her epiphany outranked her good sense, and she decided, right then and there, to postpone going to university. She was certain at that moment that she was falling in love with him and that that love would last forever. She was also certain that her parents, had they been alive, would have approved. "Seize the day," her father had so often said to her, "even the rainy ones."

That day was anything but a rainy one. Within a week, she had moved into his flat, much to her Aunt's chagrin and to Fletcher's utter delight.

Joliette did, in fact, postpone her entry into university. Indefinitely. She had decided that she wanted to start her life, let go of death and live. Really live. She had postponed that long enough already. She took up employment at the bar down the street from their flat, and aside from the small number of hours allotted to their respective jobs, the remaining were completely devoted to tender affections. They spent countless hours indulging in the trivialities of love. They wept over foreign cinema. He recited his favorite poetry to her while she soaked herself in lavender and rose petals before they made love, and she danced for him every evening, her seduction a savagery he had never before experienced. What they felt for each other was obsessive, terrifying in its intensity. Never had they felt such purity, such perfection. Never had they felt so free from expectation. Together or apart, they ached for each other, but even though the love they felt seemed beyond the bounds of reason, Joliette never had any illusions about their relationship. This was a difficult truth, a truth that tormented her soul endlessly.

"We would never be married," she woefully confessed to the darkness and to the hope held in the light just beyond it. "No," she continued, "I knew from the start. We would never have children, never have the proper flat in the proper neighborhood with the so proper jobs. But none of that mattered. I always felt hungry with him, starved without him, my heart ached at the mere thought of him. I loved him, you see. Desperately. I loved him more than I ever meant or expected to."

Three years. That was as much time as their love could abide. Three years minus one eternally dark night, the one night Fletcher failed to return home.

Joliette never heard from him again.

"Upon my bed at night, I sought him, whom my soul loves. I sought him, but found him not. I called out to him, but he gave no answer. Oh, my dear sweet ancient King," Joliette whispered to me, "That tortured lament is from the Song of Solomon. Fletcher loved that verse most of all."

So did Joliette, but the love had soured, the conviction lacked the courage to endure, and those words, they had long ceased to reassure her heart. Twenty-eight little words, Solomon's poetic words, filled with sadness and heartbreak, words that had sliced the heart of my Joliette in two. Words that Fletcher had never left her.

She clutched her legs tightly to her chest, and in the gloaming, she fell to agony and tears. As much as I wanted to comfort her, to lessen the pain of her confession, I had no means to do so, and that was more wounding than anything I had ever experienced in this life or the last.

9

Rude Awakenings *and Confrontations*

The funding board had reluctantly agreed to address Joliette this very morning regarding her implausible theory and the remote possibility of a return expedition to Kolyvan, not as an official excavation, but more of a photographic research outing in order to properly document the paintings within the tomb. Furthermore, since the data she and Botton had collected had generated more unanswered questions than it had actual facts, she was not certain they would consent to the project. Nevertheless, she felt that there was more significance to the paintings than she had been able to evaluate at that time, and if given such an opportunity, she vowed that she wouldn't rest until she uncovered the mystery of the corpse currently residing in her lab.

If she succeeded, this would be her gift to Botton, a peace offering, if you will, with deepest regrets and a concerted effort to heal old wounds. There was no other person in the whole of the world that she would rather have with her on that mountain. She, admittedly, had been a fool that night, running out on him as she had. He didn't deserve that. He had always believed in her, and she could think of no greater way to repay him for all the compromises he had made for her.

The so-called meeting turned into seven hours of grueling inquisition. Arguments were adamantly and cleverly posed, and rebuttals were offered with tact and staunch determination. Joliette was a worthy opponent, and no amount of consternation or smug looks would deter her. Joliette was a damn fine negotiator. Forgoing sleep for weeks, she had worked tirelessly writing and rewriting her *argumentum grande* with such grace, precision, and accuracy that her petition was pure unadulterated alchemy.

During the session, they pored over endless charts, graphs, and slides of the entombment, all the while my Joliette weaving the strands of her fantastic theory into an actual reality before their very eyes. The *piece de résistance* being my lovingly reconstructed face. My face would finally be unveiled in all its wondrous glory, and Joliette would be applauded with gasps and awestruck exclamations of delight. The facts might have been flimsy, but the slightest notion that they were staring into the face of a misplaced Babylonian god was too intriguing for a hasty refusal, and so they unanimously approved the funding; although, it would be a lesser endeavor, as the board had suggested a team of only four. This was a small matter of inconvenience, and as bothersome as it was, it had no untoward effect on Joliette's accelerating enthusiasm. She could just barely contain herself, so after much urgent hand shaking, cheek kissing, and congratulatory smiles, she shot off in search of Botton, thinking hopeful thoughts as she dashed across the campus.

He would be well beyond delighted. She was convinced of that, and maybe … just maybe, their two souls eclipsed by the mystical silhouette of the mountain, she could put things right between them again.

Botton was not in his lab, so she left him an insistent memo and then began the long walk to her own. She had to make a million telephone calls, and a million strategies had to be conceived and plotted if they were to depart in three months. Her mind was reeling, so naturally, as she stepped through the doorway of her lab, stumbling over her thoughts and papers in her haste, she did not see it coming. There stood Botton, leaning confidently against the lab table, engaged in an intimate almost hushed conversation with a student. A young female student. The young woman looked startled by Joliette's clumsy entrance, and at the moment their eyes met, Joliette felt the pointed chill of betrayal and its sharpened blade twist into her stomach. Exsanguinated, the blush drained from her face, and all of the documents that she had been holding fell to the floor, along with the shriveled remains of her heart. She reached down to snatch back the sense of dignity she had lost, but Botton, hearing the commotion, turned from his inglorious affair and looked over at her. The manifest guilt slapped all over his face — obvious and violating — caused Joliette to misplace the steadiness of her legs as the accusation retched from her pallid lips like vomit, "What are you doing in my lab?"

"I was waiting for you," he stammered as he attempted to put some small measure of distance between his ego and the girl. "Nicolette just happened to wander by. I was just explaining to her—"

Audibly exhaling all of the breath that remained in her body, Joliette cocked her head and assaulted Botton with a penetrating gaze forged of absolute hatred. A base, pitch-black hatred that stopped Botton from uttering one more word. His mouth hung open, and he just looked at her, looked at the emptiness in her eyes. Whatever sentiment he had hoped to cling to was, in an instant, lost to that emptiness. Joliette dropped everything in her hands and then turned abruptly and ran from the room.

Without a thought, Botton immediately gave chase, and after apprehending her in the corridor, he seized her by the arm, swinging her around to face him.

Joliette pursed her lips, and the corridor fell into an eerie silence. It was as if the walls awaited the forthcoming battle with muted anticipation.

"Jol, this isn't what it seems."

Joliette pushed her shoulders back and drew her sword. "Seems?" she replied. "This conversation seems like it's going to be a waste of my time."

"Don't do this, Jol. This is not at all what you're thinking."

"Oh, so now you propose to know what I think. How is that Olivier? In the mere two years that I have been away, did you acquire some psychic ability that I am unaware of?"

"Jol — please."

"No Olie, I am going back to Siberia."

"What?" Botton's face flushed, and his knees gave way under the weight of her words as he teetered precariously between rage, irritation, and despair. The torment on his face was not lost on Joliette, she just didn't care, and when her response came, the cold finality of steel came with it.

"There are answers there I need — that's what! Nothing more than that."

"Is that so? When did you decide this? Just now, like you always do — impulsive and angry. You nearly killed yourself last time, Jol. It's out of the question. The department will never authorize the funding anyway."

"They already have — an hour ago. So if you don't mind, you want to relax that grip on my arm."

"No, I won't. You are always running away. Were you even going to discuss this with me, Jol?"

"I was Olivier, but, in light of these recent circumstances…," she paused and looked back towards the lab and the distressed young Nicolette before continuing, "Honestly, I really don't see the point in it anymore. Do you?"

Botton had had about as much as his ego could stand, and so decisively, he attempted to throw the Herculean weight of his manhood at her. "You're not going!" he avowed with a terse mix of heroism and belligerence. "I won't allow it!"

"You won't allow it??? You won't allow it." With all the might of her will, which was substantially greater than his, she shoved him backwards until his body struck the corridor wall with a bone-crushing thud. "Olivier, I am going. No one is going to stop me. Not you. Not God himself. I will get my proof." Her anger dissipated into a fit of emotions, her words just barely audible through the tears streaming down her lovely face. "I can't stay here, Olie. We will just end up hurting each other again … that is inevitable."

The panic in Botton's eyes seized her with discomfort,

and so she sought the floor for a moment of consolation, but even the sterile vacuity of floor could not guard her from the truth.

"Damn it, Jol! Why don't you trust me? None of the rumors were true. You and I both know that. Everyone knows it. Why on earth can't you give me the benefit of the doubt. Just once?"

She lifted her gaze from the floor, and while looking through Botton's eyes directly into his soul, she replied without even a hint of emotion in her voice, "Olie, you — who know me best of all — should know the answer to that question. I only trust what the dead have to say. The living are all liars."

Her point made, she vehemently wrenched her arm from his grasp, turned, and strode off down the corridor, leaving Botton slashed to bits and speechless.

10

The Idea *that Anything is Possible*

The mountain that haunted her dreams. Jagged. Menacing. Towering against the clear blue winter sky with an unprecedented malice. Standing before her nemesis with the wind at her back, Joliette could not remember it ever being so bitter cold, so desolate, and so unforgiving. It was as if the mountain intended to deny her the very answers that she would seek, but nothing was going to stop her. The ruins of an unknown past awaited her, and sheer madness and suicidal determination impelled and guided her. Nothing short of an act of God could weaken her will, so she cast aside a trembling breath, looked to her companions for approval, and then proceeded to strap on her climbing harness.

Since the incline was treacherous and steep, covered in ice and loose rock, everything had to be hoisted up with winches. Perpetually cast in shadow, the glacial wind taunted them from every conceivable direction, and so it took a full week to get all of the camera and lighting equipment up to the summit.

After another week of organizing and reorganizing the disarray, unanimous decision among the group had affirmed that they should set up their living quarters in one of the smaller structures. This would shelter them from the hostile weather and would also allow for substantial freedom of movement in the central entombment, movement unfettered by superfluous equipment.

Although she had not made it known, this also ensured some measure of solitude in which she could explore and wrestle with her private contemplations. It was so that Joliette rarely took sleep while she was on an expedition. The sheer excitement of the undertaking worried her mind and body relentlessly, and the simple act of sketching in her journal — a meager comfort at best — was the only pursuit that gave her any solace and peace of mind.

On many a night, in the small hours of the twilight as her colleagues slept soundly, Joliette would take ease upon the inhospitable granite floor of the entombment. Alone with the darkness and her thoughts, she would scan the chaos of tumbled masonry as the shadows, lengthened and distorted by the cold florescence of the electric flood lamps, seemed to accentuate the sense of smallness she felt.

It had been two months and thirty or so nights comparable to this one that she sat randomly sketching the paintings into her leather bound record book. However, on this night, some inexplicable force repeatedly enticed her eyes away from the old paintings back to a mound of rubble on the other side of the chamber.

It was unusual, the way the rocks lay upon one another. Forced even. Not a mere act of nature, per say, but as if someone had deliberately caused an avalanche.

That theory stabbed at the neural fabric of Joliette's mind for many hours. Then, something came hurtling at her reasoning with such force that she stood up from the floor and moved cautiously to the center of the room. Once there, she changed position, slowly rotating her body to face each of the watchtowers in turn as she evaluated each wall.

North, South, East ... odd?

Each wall consisted of two columns at the center, framing within them two rows of cuneiform text and an elaborate pictograph, except the West wall, which had no text and appeared a mere pile of rubble. Now, appearances can be and oftentimes are deceiving. Joliette understood this, and so she dropped her journal, scrambled to untangle the cable of the portable lamp closest to her, and then, cable coiled over her shoulder, she ran frantically to the West wall.

Clambering up over the heap of rubble, she eventually reached a small, flat ridge, just a few meters in diameter. She crouched down to steady herself, and as she took in the heightened view of the tomb, a breath of cool air trickled upwards, chilling the back of her neck.

Fear mixed seductively with exhilaration washed over her. She felt it and shivered, teeth clenched, and as she pondered the infinite complexity of her situation, she took another deep breath. *That air.* It smelled clean and pure like fresh fallen snow. Yes. It was so obvious. The columns must have collapsed, concealing the entryway into yet another chamber. How she had overlooked this, she had no idea, but the why no longer seemed important as she considered the how. How would she get past the rubble, for they had brought with them no real excavation equipment, save her trusty pickaxe and the small sledgehammer, which dangled always dutifully at her side?

Now, Joliette was as strong in physique as she was in mind. Well above average height, she was curvaceous yet muscular. What might seem impossible to most people was more of a nuisance to Joliette. If it were her will to move rock, then the rock would have no alternative but to yield to her demands.

She slid the sledgehammer out of its holster.

Joliette had always viewed adversity as a direct challenge, and so her fury was absolute and unrivalled as she crushed to bits one mammoth fragment of rock after another. The bludgeoning iron head of the sledgehammer drove thunderclaps six-feet into her skull and sent shrapnel flying to the heavens with each stroke. Shards of rock nicked her face and frayed the flesh on her hands, and yet after working tirelessly for hours, she still felt energized. She couldn't stop, not until she felt enough space had been fashioned in the rock. Just enough that she might possibly ease her body into the fracture.

When she was certain, she dropped the sledgehammer to the ground at her feet, took hold of the portable flood lamp, and shone it into the crevice. The yawning chasm bared its teeth and devoured the light, but even so, she could still barely make out the steep inclined plane of what again appeared to be a corridor, which eventually widened and spiraled downward.

But the hole she had made in the rock was tight. She

immediately realized this and that she would not make it through with the added bulk of her parka, so she unzipped and quickly cast aside her clothing until she was relieved of all but her trousers and an undershirt. Open to the elements, steam rose, swirling out and away from her body as her skin hit the frigid air. Instantly deadened from the cold, her flesh went numb and pale, apart from her hands, which were red and raw, set ablaze from lacerations gifted by the infuriated rock. So she rubbed her hands together for a moment to ease the pain, and then she took up the slack in the flood lamp's electrical cable, slid it into the hole, and gradually lowered it down into the corridor until it confirmed bottom.

It took a while. The bottom did not rise up to meet her for the corridor was steep and obstructed, but it was a short run, maybe five or so meters at the most. Joliette's heart leapt with delight. A measly five meters. This she could manage. She crouched down to the floor and slid her right shoulder into the crack, gently, readjusting her position ever so slightly here and there as jagged shards of rock bit and tore at her exposed flesh. It was a little bit tighter than she had estimated, but, Joliette was far too numb to take notice of the pain, and undaunted by the rock's overt resistance, she slowly counted down from three and exhaled the very last wisp of breath left in her lungs, compressing her chest until it ached. "Time to chase another dragon down the hole, and this time," she declared, "I'm going to catch it."

The good-humored taunt had given her all the confidence she needed to wrench her torso through the crack, but a lack of confidence was the least of her problems. The rock was slick from the damp air, and so the fall was quick but no less painful as her head smacked into the cold, hard certainty of the granite floor beneath. Stunned for the moment, she could do little but gaze up fixedly into the twilight. Into the vault of the ceiling, which was beyond view or imagination, and the longer she stared into it, the more it appeared exposed. Tiny sparks of light twinkled far off in the distance as if the evening sky had punched through the icy mountaintop. She could smell and taste the coolness of water.

Water?

She took several deep breaths in an attempt to stop the dizziness, rolled over, and drew herself up onto her knees. In that moment, staring at the little symbols carved into the floor beneath her body, an overpowering sense of *déjà vu* slammed into Joliette. She felt as if she had stood in this very place before. Stared at these very symbols. Yes. She had. The tomb in Anatolia. It was a perfect negative image of this tomb. Identical in its every aspect. Pyramidal in its geometry, equal in size, and yet, this tomb was filled with all of the trappings that she had expected in the other but had been denied. She lifted the fallen flood lamp from the floor and cast its glow to the heavens, illuminating a sepulcher expansive in its architecture.

At the midpoint of the chamber was a towering basalt altar, flanked on two sides by massive winged titans. Grotesque, mutated beasts they were, ferocious and cruel, bearing down upon her with the broad sinewed bodies of oxen and the heavily tattooed heads of temple sentinels. Crowned with bejeweled spikes, they stared down at her with wild and confrontational eyes. A mote, nourished by water from the blackest of seas, surrounded the altar, reflecting the beasts' hostile warning from every conceivable angle. The vast inky pools, several meters in length, lay between the altar and the ominous beasts. The water's oily surface shimmered in the feeble light of the lamp, betraying its depth and purpose, but Joliette knew. She knew that the future and the past lingered there, foretold in the glistening obsidian.

Threatening her resolve with a cold inanimate savagery, the great titans fixed their hard hollow eyes upon her, but oddly, Joliette found that she felt no hesitation at all. She moved through the murky water, fearless. Almost gliding towards the altar, her footsteps cast not a single ripple upon its surface. She didn't exist here. Didn't exist anywhere, and yet, here she was. So close now. The stillness, maddening. One step away, one step, one breath at a time, she climbed out of the water and began her ascent up the steps, and upon reaching the summit, she stood there, still and awestruck before the altar, her hands trembling at her sides.

After brushing the dirt from its cover, Joliette noticed that the altar's lid, splintered in three places, lay precariously askew. Without much force or effort, she managed to shift the smaller pieces, and crashing to the floor in a swirl of dust and debris, they fell away, exposing its inner recesses. Inside, amidst the grit, gravel, and lichen, a finely carved alabaster jar rested on its side. Its seal, from what Joliette could detect, had not been violated. The contents must still be intact. The thought seemed plausible, but plausible had often betrayed her, so she had to be certain. She reached into the crypt, cautious, placing her hands gently upon the jar. Surprisingly, it felt slick, like glazed porcelain, yet unnaturally warm to the touch, and the dust covering its surface seemed charged with static. As she wrapped her hands around the jar, tiny sparks of light began radiating from her fingertips, slowly surging an electro-static charge through her body.

More so a reflex than fear of dropping it, she gripped the jar tighter, and in that moment, all the energy of my soul in its entirety passed through and into her with a violent force. It threw her back from the crypt and down the altar stairs. Before she could catch her breath and any sense of logic, the obsidian pools ignited in flame, setting the chamber ablaze in luminous shades of saffron and indigo, releasing my memories from the darkness.

Joliette couldn't move. The impact had jarred her loose from the physical world. She couldn't speak beyond a whimper, and she couldn't surmount the inconceivable chasm that had opened in her mind.

Powerful were the myths emblazoned upon the walls of this tomb. Vague and long forgotten myths and memories. Corrupted by the decay of ages and laid to waste beneath the disparaging constancy of the mountain, still, the images clung tenaciously to their glory. Each slight and delicate nuance of light and shadow had, while faded, remained persistent during the engulfing eons of obscurity. The memory of me had persisted. I had persisted, and so invoking the raw power of all that once was tangible, I appeared to her — a mere apparition — a figment of my own imagination, conjured up from the dust of time and knitted together from its savage stillness and its soulless empty spaces.

Still clutching the alabaster jar, Joliette regained her footing and gazed back at me, unafraid, embracing the idea of me as if I were true of form and matter. "What is this place?" she asked, moving towards me, her breath just barely tinted with mist.

"It is a book, my love, the basalt pages of a great and

ancient book of prophecy, etched into the very core of the world."

"What prophecy?"

"Behold, my beloved, Joliette. Behold the birth of a King and the ascension of a God. A story once legend now lost to this hollow place in time."

As Joliette studied the eidolons imprinted upon the walls, the chamber began to spin. The images in flux, the colors vibrant, they shimmered, iridescent, as if the rock still leached the blood of the peoples who had painted them. As the story unfolded, there arose the figure of a humble man crowned as King. He sat upon a majestic steed, drawing his mighty bow with courage and truth. Thousands of devotees rained praise upon him as he awarded them all the many bountiful gifts of his lands.

He spoke only the words of truth,

And his people prospered.

He spoke only the words of poetry,

And his people loved.

He spoke only the words of love,

And his people rose to might.

Upon his death, the gods showered his body with tears and whispered their secrets to the ether so that he might ascend to his rightful place among them. Sentinels and heavily armored warriors vigilantly tended to their almighty sovereign. For there were battles to be fought in the afterlife, with swords forged of lightening and flame, and victories that would eclipse all truth in the world.

As my history, the history of her beloved King, unfolded before her eyes, Joliette's mind twisted. So many unanswered questions plagued her that her consciousness was on the verge of violent collapse. She did her best to resist its demise with logic. "Wait, this can't be," she exclaimed. "I see many boats braving the treachery of the Black Sea, and the towering obsidian temple, hidden deep within the Anatolian mountains … why? Why did they secret you away, what purpose could it have possibly served? It doesn't make any sense."

"To protect me, of course," I replied. "It makes perfect sense. My flesh was to endure forever in the temple of my everlasting body."

"And this place?"

"The temple of my immortal Soul, that which you now hold in your hands, my beloved Joliette."

In disbelief and astonishment, Joliette looked down upon the jar she still held gently in her hands. Her legs began trembling. Her heart felt weak. Her breath, strained, and her head whirled with a million dizzying sensations of light and truth. She felt faint, unworthy of the power she held at her fingertips, and so the strength of her will, long ago borrowed from the rock, began to fail her. She collapsed under the weight of her sins, and as her fading body lay defeated in my arms, I whispered the poetry of my name to comfort her soul, "It is time, my beloved. I am nothing, and I am all things. My secrets are now yours to know, as only you can know them. I always knew that you would come for me, would find me, when you needed to. Now it's time to release your heart and release your soul… "

Stay with me forever, my love. All things end and then begin again. I will love you always. Believe in me, if nothing else. Believe in our love and stay with me now. Joliette … my darling Joliette. Stay with me. I love you.

Will love you. Forever and always…

And the only word Joliette could manage to whisper in return before oblivion took her was, "Yes."

In that one word, I felt every agony that had ever tormented her soul, and even though I wanted that 'yes' to be for me, it was not. Even though I yearned to be the one to whisper those words to her in the darkness, I was not the one who did. Indeed, how I wished those words were mine, but they were not, and I felt the ache of that realization. Felt it so deeply that in my desperation, I commanded the earth to quake.

11

When a Memory *becomes more than a Dream*

J oliette? Turn your head please and look at me now. Yes, that's it. Try to focus. Do you have any idea where you are? My name is Doctor Deaufant," said the woman in the white coat as she moved the penlight back and forth over Joliette's eyes. "Can you hear me, Joliette?"

If Joliette had had half a mind, she would have responded with an irritated, 'Hear what? The incessant babbling of a clueless Doctor,' and no one would have taken issue with her sarcasm. With all the technology at their disposal, one might wonder why a medical professional would ask such an absurd question, especially to someone who had no capacity to answer rationally. Joliette hadn't the vaguest inkling under God where she was. The light shining in her eyes was blinding, and she responded with one word. The only word that came into her mind, "Kolyvan?"

"Bon! Tres Bon," replied the doctor. "She is going to be just fine. I will be back in a few hours to check on her. Keep talking to her, it will wake her mind."

Botton gave an appreciative nod to the doctor before she left the room. After she had gone, he leant over, brushed the unruly tendrils of hair from Joliette's forehead, and whispered a few soft words of encouragement into her ear, "Joliette, can you hear me? It's me. Olivier. You're back in Toulouse now. You're going to be just fine. Stay with me. Please, Jol. Just stay with me."

The room, its stark severity was overwhelming, and an acrid stench hung in the air. An antiseptic stench, assaulting her airways, burning her eyes, and there was a deep numbness that had crept into her left arm. It felt disconnected from the rest of her body, and so she couldn't move it for all her effort. It looked pale, deathly pale but for the entrance of the needle where there it had leached an angry spot of blood onto the bandage as it violated the vein in her hand. Her mind felt blurred, lost to her, her thoughts, distant, and through the fugue, she could just barely hear the muffled, almost distant hum of the machines, murmuring insistently to one another. Clicking and buzzing away in their surreptitious computerized language. Monitoring all things vital, she supposed.

"Hospital?"

"Yes, hospital," Botton confirmed, thoroughly relieved that she had heard him through the medicated haze. His shoulders relaxed, and he sat back down in his chair. "You know, I don't know how you do it. There is more of your blood in that tomb than anyone else's. What on earth were you thinking, Jol?"

Botton didn't really need her to answer. He knew her too well. She hadn't been thinking. That was the problem. In her alleged suicidal haste to gain entry to my sanctuary, her sledgehammer had left razor sharp edges to the surrounding rock. Anesthetized from the cold, she had not taken notice of its blade as it ripped through her flesh, tearing open the artery in her arm during her tumble down into the chamber. Were it not for the acute hypothermia and the generator cable for the floodlight, her comrades would not have found her in time. Although, I have to give credit to myself for the minor earthquake. Someone had to wake them up.

Urging her to rest and be quiet with the tenderest of admonishments, Botton looked splendid seated before her. The light glinting ever so slightly off his dark hair revealed an unassuming humility, and although his face was sallow and weary from long tormented and sleepless nights, his was the only face that Joliette wished to look upon. She acknowledged his affection with a gentle squeeze of her free hand. She missed holding his hand, but there were too many unanswered questions to remain quiet. "I found him, Olie. There is something in the crypt. Everything is so fuzzy, detached, but I remember. The way it felt. I held it in my hands."

"I know," he confirmed as the tears thickened in his eyes. "I always knew that you would. We have a full team there now. It is a remarkable discovery, Jol. Apparently, his people had been waiting. Thousands of years. Waiting to reunite his body with his spirit. The entire rite is written on the walls in what appears to be blood mixed with all sorts of exotic pigments. It's…" Botton smiled, and in hopes of avoiding notice and potential embarrassment, he swiftly wiped the tears from his cheek with the back of his shaking hand. "It's unbelievable is what it is."

"In the crypt, Olie, the phylactery. What was in it?"

"A heart," he quickly answered, indulging her anxiety. "Still steeped in bitumen, along with some strange amulets and jewelry."

"Olie, you can't let anyone take it. It belongs with his body. We must … we must get it here at once!"

"Relax, Jol. I have taken care of it. It's on its way. You need to calm down. You don't have the energy yet to be going on like this. I am glad you are awake, finally, but don't make me call for a sedative, ok? I've taken care of everything."

As anxious as she was, confused and disoriented, his confident words soothed and centered her agitated mind. She knew that she should never have doubted him. "You always know precisely what's on my mind. I don't know what I would do without you, Olie."

"I do. You would go off like a raving lunatic, pickaxe soaring high over your head, shouting Holy Grail nonsense while flinging yourself off the sides of mountains or throwing yourself down some dank hole in the earth. Just relax now, Jol. You can tell me everything … later. I'm going to get some coffee and make a few telephone calls. Let everyone know that you're awake. I won't be a moment, all right?"

She nodded and resigned herself with a sigh.

"Stay quiet now. I mean it," he said as he kissed her softly on the lips. She smiled up at him and placed a pale, cool hand upon his cheek. He closed his eyes and yielded to her caress, if only for a moment.

"Olie — your face!?"

Startled by her abrupt declaration, Botton pulled

away. He stepped back from the bed and reflexively put his own hands to his face in an attempt to reason away her hysterics. Once he had, he realized what had confused her. "Ah. I shaved it off. Too much trouble." He rubbed his hand over his hairless chin as if he were sorting through some equally perplexing mathematical conundrum, one to which there was no solution. "Hey, didn't I tell you to be quiet? Anyway, I don't know how I feel about it yet."

"What's not to know? It brightens your smile. I love it, Olie. Really. Stop obsessing."

Hers was a warm accepting logic, a logic he had come to know so well, so he shook a finger at her in jest and smiled back while declaring that "Coffee!" was the more important matter at hand. With his intent firmly planted in his mind, Botton exited the room, and Joliette settled down into the sheets, closed her wearied eyes, and pushed her mind back to the tomb.

It was not a hallucination.

His words still rang out clear in her mind, and she had felt his unmistakable touch upon her skin. His hand pressing into her own. No, it was not a hallucination.

As her mind eventually began to drift off with sleep, she could feel herself sinking down into the obsidian pool. Its water, cool and revitalizing. He had stood before her. Her great Babylonian god. Her King, fallen from the starlit sky. His gaze, as indistinct as his reflection in the water, had somehow penetrated the very depths of her being. Penetrated the veil of lies obscuring her most secret desires, and as the black water rippled against her face, she understood the realities of love. This love. All love. And that understanding filled her with a sense of peace and tranquility the likes of which she had so longed for.

In a moment, he had known her, and in a moment, one so rare in a lifetime, she knew his name. A name that stole from her mind in an almost inaudible whisper, and her thoughts heard, were answered. A voice, laden with heartbreak and anguish, sang sweetly to her from the subconscious depths of her memory, "Who is this that comes towards me out of the smoke in the wilderness? Thou art all fair my love…"

"…and there is no flaw in you," she answered back from her dream. A dream, decayed, covered in the rubble of a life. The dream she had so long tried to suppress barely disturbed the air as the breath of his name slid from her lips, "Fletcher?"

"Yes, it's me," came the hesitant reply. With that reply, Joliette's pulse quickened, rushing her urgently from her dream, and her eyes shot open, but she didn't know whether or not to trust them. She blinked her eyelids frantically in an attempt to stave off the burn, but even through the blur of moisture and the exasperating glare of the room clouding her vision, she could see that it was indeed, Fletcher. A bit tatty at the edges, but it seemed time had been kind to him, and in spite of a few wayward grey hairs, the sparkle in his eye had not lost its luster. He was just as handsome as he had been the day she met him on the train. "How did you find me?" she asked.

"Well, you are a quite the celebrity these days." He held up the newspaper so that she could read the headline: TOULOUSIAN ARCHAEOLOGIST ALMOST DIES DURING MONUMENTAL EXCAVATION IN KOLYVAN. "It's all over the news, Jolie. You were in cardiac arrest when they found you. The doctors told me that you damn near bled to death. Reckless." He shook his head. "You were always so damn reckless."

To the chaotic rhythm of his words, Fletcher gently caressed the back of her hand with his thumb, but I could sense that the tenderness was more of a nervous gesture, however cleverly disguised, and as drained as she was by her ordeal, the pain in Joliette's heart still felt sharp to her. "I died twenty years ago," she said. "You left me alone to die. I was reckless for loving you."

"I know, Jolie, and I am truly sorry for that. But it was you who once adamantly declared that I wasn't a liar, despite my conviction to the contrary. You knew me best of all, and you were absolutely right. I couldn't live a lie. Still can't. A thief is a poor substitute for a husband."

"You couldn't be a poor substitute for anything, and we had something, didn't we Fletcher? We had true love?"

"No. The only truth in it was that we were in love with the idea of us. It was a dream Jolie. Just a wonderful dream."

Joliette had had many a dream over the course of her life. If their love had been a dream, it felt cruel and heartless, and Joliette could bear no more. Her body had been beaten down, her soul was exhausted, and the walls of stone that she had so carefully erected around her heart fell crumbling into dust at his feet. There was nothing left to hold back the sadness, so when the tears came, they poured out in choking sobs in spite of herself.

Fletcher could not recall a time when she had ever shed tears in front of him, and in his noticeable state of uneasiness, he made an imprudent attempt to change the topic of discourse. "So, this French bloke, he loves you very much. Don't have to be cupid to figure that one out. He's barely left this room in six weeks. You love him, Jolie. I know you do. I heard the way you said his name while you were sleeping. I only ever wanted the best for you. It was never in the cards for us, and I am sure that he will make you happy."

As much as he had hoped that total surrender would make things right, he knew in his heart that nothing could justify a delusion of that magnitude. Even I could feel the anger as it swelled inside of her — a festering malice — eating her alive from the inside out. She wanted nothing more than to be rid of it, but she scarcely had the strength to release it. "What?" she shouted with as much intensity as she could muster. "Is that the best you've got? You really are a sadistic bastard. Yes, Bastard. I said it. Lying, thieving, bastard! Is that extreme enough for you? Fuck' sake Fletcher, why did you come here — to gloat, to torture me — what?"

"No. Of course not. I would never … I came here because I owe you an explanation, at the very least."

"At the very least, that's noble. A noble thief, and you pick now, twenty years of agony later. I would've thought stealing it was enough for you. So just how many times are you going to break my heart?"

"I am hoping only this once," he confessed with every ounce of passion he could dredge from within, desperately hoping that she would take pity on him and spare him her wrath. He leant in and kissed her on the lips, but the sweetness, the taste of her anger, cut him to the quick. "You look as beautiful as you did on the day I first set my eyes on you. And not that it matters to you, Jolie, but my heart broke that day as well." Fletcher reached into the pocket of his overcoat and pulled out an old, tattered paperback. He set it down next to her on the bedside table. "I believe that this belongs to you," he continued while making a solemn turn towards the door.

"I have kept it long enough."

Faced with his departure, Joliette could not decide how she felt in that moment or which affected more pain than the other. Watching him leave or having been denied her witness the first time. "Au revoir, mon amour," was as much as her breath would allow for a last plaintive plea, but the words just clung to her lips — stale and filled with despair — as he walked out of the room without the slightest hesitation.

Botton returned a moment later, clutching two cups of coffee and a bottle of water. Caught completely off-guard by her sobbing, the rouge slipped away from his face. Granted, it was an overly emotional day for everyone, but he knew that he had not left her in this sorry state. He strove to remain calm in his confusion. "Jol, what's wrong?" he said in the most soothing tone of voice he could find, and as he reached out to place the coffee cups down on the bedside table, he noticed the wayward paperback and lifted it up.

The Collected Works of Oscar Wild?

Botton thought it odd, though he couldn't place any logic behind it without plumbing the depths of his own recollections. He pondered the title silently for a moment, but the lack of connection only frustrated him more. He knew that he had not placed it there. That fact was undisputable, and with that realization, an unexpected chill moved over his flesh. He hastily glanced around the room so as not to be surprised by an errant visitor or overzealous nurse. Then, somewhat satisfied with the perceived sense of privacy, he commenced flipping through the volume, stopping quite abruptly upon its title page. There, in a watered-down splotch of ink, lay the enigmatic inscription: Illusion is the first of all pleasures.

Remember me fondly, my love.

"Zut Alors," the exclamation fell from his mouth as accidentally as the book fell from his hands. Botton turned, looked at the door as if it were made of iron bars, and then proceeded to bolt from the room out into a corridor that seemed endless, and so the figure he sought, who was stepping into the elevator, seemed a thousand miles away. As the distance stretched out before him, the air suddenly stopped moving. His body stopped moving, and time itself stopped moving as a stifled breath tore from his chest, "Fletcher!?"

Botton could not believe that that name had entered his mind, let alone left off his lips with such pronouncement. If, in fact, it did turn out to be Fletcher, what would he do? Should he punch him in the face or maybe challenge him to a duel? Ah! How he would love to run him through with a sharpened sword, to watch his entrails spill from the open wound. To watch him bleed out knowing the agony was just punishment. Such a treacherous cad deserved nothing less in his opinion. The anger Botton felt swelled and burned under his skin, and judgment raced through his mind with intense, though premature, satisfaction.

In reply to Botton's outburst, the figure stopped abruptly, stepped back from the elevator, and remained in sullen acknowledgement, head bowed low as if strung from the gallows. Eyes swollen. Stained crimson with misery and regret.

Feeling confident that he had the upper hand, Botton sauntered up to Fletcher, taking a Machiavellian stance as he waited for just the right moment to run him through, but upon witnessing the man's tears, the eloquent expression of rage that Botton had rehearsed tirelessly was lost to him. Even the cold, icy stare, that which he had planned to assault Fletcher with, melted away into compassion, and so the two men stood face to face in grief and confusion.

"Joliette spoke of you often in the desert," Botton affirmed kindly out of a gnawing respect for the man's obvious pain. "We love her. Don't we?" he continued, and Fletcher's reply fell to the floor, as the shame that had overcome him was too great to allow him to look Botton in the eyes.

"Yes, we do," he confessed.

Requisite empathy taken into account, Botton was not about to be swayed by this man's impoverished soul. He wanted closure, and he would have it. "Eight long years, I have been living with the ghost of you," he said with renewed contempt. "She is in love with you. She blamed herself. You left her with nothing. Not even a word. How can you leave her again?"

"I can't give her what she needs," Fletcher replied. "She knows that." And as he prepared to further explain, he fixed Botton with a hardened look directly into his eyes. "I loved her more than I should have, more than I thought was possible, and more than I ever intended to, but love doesn't change anything. She has a gift. She had a life ahead of her, and my life, such as it is, doesn't suit anyone but me. You, on the other hand ... you can give her everything, and she loves you as well. You just need to tell her how you feel."

"I have," said Botton, the reluctant disclosure stumbling from his mouth before he had a mind to check it. "But she just ... she just pushes me away."

"Well now," Fletcher countered, "then you didn't take the proper tack with her, did you? It's really that simple."

For Botton, nothing was ever simple, and so he couldn't stop his body from wilting in defeat. Drained of all arrogance and vigor, Botton finally felt the futility his heart had known for some time, and Fletcher's angry reply would lash out at his weakened ego. Botton could do little but wince at its sting. "'She doesn't love me that way?' 'It's no use?' Ah, bloody hell, you Frenchmen make me sick. Always touting yourselves as the world's most fabulous lovers. That's a gas isn't it? Considering you've all got your heads half way up your asses all the time. Joliette is not the sort of woman who needs or wants to be asked permission," Fletcher continued. "It's pathetic. Take her if you want her. Eight years? What are you waiting for?" Fletcher presented his back to Botton in disgust and stepped assuredly into the elevator. As the doors began to close, he turned and abruptly shot out his hand to stop them. He looked the defeated Botton square in the eyes and made a final plea for mercy, "I know that I might be asking too much of you, Frenchman, but take care with her. Her armor shimmers, but it's thin. Don't ever say I didn't warn you."

Struck with an unfamiliar sense of bewilderment, Botton nodded in acceptance, and Fletcher withdrew his hand, allowing the elevator doors to proffer the closure that they both required.

Shaken, yet profoundly impressed by Fletcher's eloquent and truthful words, Botton took a moment to brush himself off and then promptly returned to Joliette.

Upon entering the room, he was delighted to find that her entire disposition had changed dramatically in the twenty or so odd minutes he had been gone. She looked so lovely and calm, as if the burden she had carried for an eternity had finally been lifted. The darkness in her eyes seemed faded as they moved over him as he approached the bed. How he loved the unhurried, contemplative way she looked at him, and so he slid the chair in closer, sat down, and before weighing up one word, he clasped her hand in his.

Now, Botton had never been the sort of man who was eager to express his feelings, nevertheless, he made a valiant start, "Joliette, there are too many things I should have said to you that I have not said, too many things I should have done that I have not done, and far too many things I did that I am ashamed of…"

Botton would have continued by declaring how badly he wanted her and how he felt as if he couldn't breathe when he was near her, but in an effort to spare him, Joliette interjected, for she was not the sort of woman who would take satisfaction in his apparent discomfort. Didn't matter though, Botton needed this moment more than he needed her sympathy.

"No, Joliette. Let me finish, please."

"Damn it, Olie, you always have to make things so difficult. Why can't you just say what you need?"

"Fine," he said in an urgent and pointed whisper, which gradually took on a much firmer tenor. "I'll take that tone of yours to mean that I have permission to speak boldly here. Six weeks of silence, and I have had some time to think, so what I need, Jol — the truth — what I need is an answer. I know things are never this simple, not for us, but for now, I need it to be. Yes or no? Don't you feel anything for me? Anything at all? Do you love me, hate me? Do you want me at all? Oh, damn it to hell, Joliette. Despite what you might think, I am not going to leave you. Not now. Not ever. I just don't know what it's going to take."

Botton wanted to press further, but his heart sank when she told him to shut up. He sucked in a breath and looked to Joliette, expecting the stern, disciplinarian air that she had so often afforded him as companion to those words, but in its place, the look gracing her lovely face was not at all what he had anticipated. She was smiling at him. A deep affectionate smile that lit up her entire face. A smile he knew in his heart was for no one else but him. Botton's entire body gave way to relief. He had waited eight long years for that smile, and he was thankful that he had. He kissed the back of her hand and then pressed it to his face. "All right then," he said as he returned the gesture with his own wide mouthful of teeth. "Isn't love grand?"

"Oui." Joliette nodded in agreement. "It is my love. It most certainly is."

With that, Botton stood up, flung one hand into the air, put one foot on the seat of his chair, cleared his throat with authority, and then began carrying on quite gallantly, or rather, carrying on as any idiot would considering the unbearable lightness he felt in his heart, *"L'amour est le printemps...,"* he declared in a tenuous love-struck voice, *"Et toi, mon p'tit chou ... tu es le soleil."*

Ridiculous is a Frenchman in love. Worse, an intellectual Frenchman with only a rudimentary knowledge of love's poetry.

Joliette found the spectacle to be just as ridiculous, but it was pointless to try to rein him in, so she simply shook her head and gave him a willful grin.

"Don't push it now, Olie."

12

The Splendor of Antiquity

Contrary to my original belief, some things do not die. Although Fletcher never returned, his love for Joliette endured, and she would honor his request of her always, remembering him often and fondly. The love they had shared was forever etched into the history of their lives. Flawless and unchangeable.

At this particular juncture of the narrative, I feel compelled to make a public apology to Olivier Botton. My love for Joliette had tainted my viewpoint, and I had judged him quite unfairly. He was an honorable man. For eight years, from the moment he made love to Joliette under the stars in India, he had neither want nor wish to entertain any other. His undying passion for her extended well beyond his egotistical façade, and his intentions towards her had never been anything less than virtuous, unlike the jealous and slanderous words that I had viciously set upon him.

Joliette and Botton resolved their feelings for one another that very day in the hospital, and, in fact, they did live happily ever after.

They would continue to labor together for three exhaustive years, researching the intricacies of my mythological existence. As aggressive as they were towards each other, the constant challenge only improved their stamina. Botton would eventually work out the infinite ambiguities of my sword, and Joliette would later decipher the cuneiform funeral rite in its entirety. Together, they would spend many months touring the university lecture circuit, sharing their knowledge and findings with the entire archaeological world.

However, despite all of the accolades and notable mentions, a laboratory, with its sterile chill, can be an unrealized prison for minds of a certain persuasion. Joliette longed desperately for the open sky, and so at Botton's request, they returned to Kolyvan, where the scale and ethereal beauty of the landscape hurled Botton into a state of rapture as soon as he set his eyes upon it. The windswept grasses, dotted with thousands of violet and magenta twilights, spread out before him, and Joliette began to run towards the mountain. The sunlight reflecting off of the blaze of gold in her hair and the way the wildflowers pushed up against her as she ran, in all his years drifting the globe, he had never before witnessed such awe-inspiring majesty, and for the first time in his life, he felt the earth beneath his feet.

Inevitably, restraint forged of fear weakens. Botton's emotions eventually broke free, and as all ridiculous Frenchmen in love feel compelled to do, he pronounced his love to Joliette in a most splendid and grandiose fashion. Down on one knee, atop the altar of my soul. For as far as Botton was concerned: Love was the springtime, and Joliette was indeed the sun.

Upon their return from Kolyvan, they married in Toulouse and subsequently relocated back to Joliette's beloved adoptive home, the London borough of Harrow, where, after a lengthy honeymoon respite, Joliette accepted a prominent research position at the famed British Museum, and Botton, a professorship at Oxford.

My timeless journey, on the other hand, would not reach its conclusion in Toulouse. I would accompany Joliette and Botton to London as well, and much to my surprise, the British museum was not the horrid state of imprisonment I had once assumed that it would be. For you see, Joliette, alchemist and divine conjurer, had succeeded in reuniting matter with spirit. Through her love and devotion for the idea of me, she shared my face with the world. My history would be forever chronicled as legend. The legend of her beloved King. The legend of a God among men.

Before this tale comes to its finish, one incident remains that warrants mention. Joliette's vision. If such an inexplicable thing did happen, then one must be prepared to accept the inevitability of the cosmos and one must also accept its chaos, its order, and one's own place in it. Now, for most scientists, the tangible often gets in the way, but mercifully, it does not for my Joliette. Certainly scores of individuals have dreamt far stranger things while wandering the naked and uncharted depths of twilight's abyss. They might dream of contorted, distorted things. An alternate reality, perhaps, one composed of unrelated bits and pieces of daily life. Events. Places. A sea of familiar and unfamiliar faces. A disjointed array of words spoken and words thought yet unspoken. All this detritus might wind up haphazardly muddled together and then subsequently rearranged into fantastic and oftentimes frightening forms by an unchecked subconscious. Joliette, however, steadfastly denied this argument, as she had always believed, without the slightest reservation, that she had been sane and awake during her ordeal and that the awakening of the beasts and the black pool flames she had experienced in my sanctuary on that particular evening was majesty that had be witnessed by no one before her. Thus, she concluded that the incident could not merely be dismissed as trauma induced hallucination. This hypothesis seemed reasonable to Joliette. In her mind, that line of reasoning was clearly borne out by the curious and inexplicable depth of understanding that she now possessed regarding her love for me, my love for her, and the enduring love she and Botton felt for one another, which had continued to strengthen over the years, despite the deliberate lack of encouragement on their part.

Through endless dusks and eternal dawns, Joliette had dreamt and waited, allowing loneliness and grief to eat away at her soul. Eventually, the shadow of solitude broke her, and her desperate longing for the light of love grew so wild and reckless that her heart could rest no more. One's heart can neither be denied nor overcome, no matter how tirelessly one fights to defeat it. When she fell for Botton, it was a fall from a most precipitous height. She had tried to deny her own feelings in an effort to spare her heart further pain, but her excuses, many and elaborate, were undeniably worthless.

Botton also came to understand all of this. For in the search for definitive proof, he had made a grave miscalculation in underestimating the powers of the universe. The infinite machinations of the cosmos rarely avail themselves to an arrogant mind, as mystery has but one desire. It simply wishes to be embraced for what it is, nothing more. His love for Joliette required no logical justifications or mathematically validating principles.

One mystery would remain, however. Although Joliette knew my name, as I had whispered it to her in the darkness, she never once breathed it to the world. You see, Joliette truly believed in mystery, and to the end of her days, she would continue to impress that a world without mystery nurtures a shallow existence. An empty quest devoid of life where all the hope and promise of discovery have been forsaken for fact. She believed that an existence without intangibles was mournfully without passion and love.

My name would be our secret memory.

My memories had become her memories.

Her memories had become mine,

And ours would forever belong to the Splendor of Antiquity

About the Author

Cheryl Anne Gardner is a writer of dark, often disturbing art-house novellas and abstract flash fiction. Her love of literature began at an early age with Stoker's Dracula. Captivated by the Gothic and Dark Romantic stylings of Poe, Lovecraft, Kafka, and de Sade, her passion for the macabre manifests itself throughout her own work to this day. In 2010, she became enamoured with Flash Fiction and its experimental style, and she's been writing prolifically in the genre ever since. She enjoys exploring political, social, and psychological issues. Her flash fiction has been published in dozens of journals. When she isn't writing, she likes to chase marbles on a glass floor, eat lint, play with sharp objects, and make taxidermy dioramas with dead flies. She lives with her husband on the east coast USA, is an enthusiastic gardener, and dabbles in cement sculpture when she isn't spoiling her adopted feral cats.

You can find her work at various online retailers. Her novellas are available in print and in eBook formats.

Titles by Cheryl Anne Gardner

Knowing Joe
Kitsch
The Duskhouse
And Death Dreamt Us All
The Thin Wall
The Kissing Room
Logos

You wanted transcendence, wanted height, danger, the tracks blurred into murky distances behind and in front of you. You slipped, reached for it, starlight shining in your eyes, something you didn't have when I held your hand.

We didn't fold the laundry this morning, or straighten the tussled sheets. I picked up the mail, but you never opened it.

Yesterday you forgot to buy the raspberry tart I love so much, and I forgot the green tea with jasmine you drink from that old flowery teacup I broke last week and didn't tell you about.

How could I forget your eyes are blue, the concrete beneath you, dingy, muddled with oil.

I hold your hand now and wonder if you can hear me; was there ever a moment you could?

I suspect there was, but there's blood in your hair, and I'm sorry …

I'm sorry for everything: for you, for me, for us.